In this big-hearted paean to the absurdity of small town life, Don Hurd has written a comic Texas masterpiece.

Steven L Davis
Author of *Texas Literary Outlaws*

Combining the processed meat-like texture of the works of Vonnegut and the astute comedic absurdity of the McRib, Don Hurd creates an instant counterculture classic that's slathered in barbecue sauce and only available when pork prices are low.

Paddy Carrillo
Author of *Wasteoid Daydream*

I0548313

Prairie Oysters

A Novel

Don Hurd

Toad Press
2015

ISBN 978-0692454121
ISBN 0692454128
A portion of this book appeared in
Southwestern American Literature
and *New Stories from the Southwest*

Author's Note

It was Steven L. Davis, my literary compadre, who first read a short story titled "The Only Show in Town" and suggested it might make a good novel. I resisted this idea for some time. I had what I thought was a perfectly good short story in the bag and the idea of writing a novel was not especially appealing to me. In the end, Steve convinced me and I will always be grateful. Thanks also to Russell Hoke who read and helped proof the book in several drafts, including a memorable night when we read the novel in its entirety only to have the pages swept away by a strong wind after the sun came up. I will always recall fondly the two of us chasing manuscript pages across the yard.

Special thanks to my wife Irma and my two sons Armand and Ezra for putting up with me during the composition of this novel when I was sleep-deprived and intolerably grumpy.

Lastly, I want to thank Otto Furst, the hero of "The Only Show in Town," who disappeared from the book when he was ruthlessly supplanted by Melchor Mendoza. He deserved better.

For Lucy and Glen

Prologue

A cloud passed over the face of the moon, darkening the waters of the Espantosa. A ragged mist crept slowly across the lake, gathering to form hieroglyphics, weaving a tale of past and present so large that only the lake could tell it.

No one was there to witness the mystery of that incantation, nor, had anyone been present, would it have been understood.

Chapter One

On the morning Miss Amanda Coakely drove her battered yellow Dodge into Espantosa, Guadalupe Lopez noticed her father's milagro nopal was dying. The cactus was more than a hundred years old and had followed the fortunes of the Lopez family from Guadalajara to Laredo to Shiner, Uvalde, Brackettville, and, finally, Espantosa. With each successive move a piece of the venerable succulent was cut and ceremoniously replanted when the family arrived at their destination. When Guadalupe's father, Hilario, arrived in Espantosa, he took one look at the inhospitable soil and shook his head.

"If this pigheaded nopal can grow here," he commented, "it will be a miracle."

For a time it seemed that the nopal would finally succumb. Hilario's fortunes too seemed to have taken a turn for the worse. Work was hard to come by. To complicate matters, his wife was pregnant with Guadalupe. Her diet was so poor he worried she would not be able to produce milk for the baby when it arrived. Then Hilario walked out one morning to find the cactus had put forward a tiny tuna. He raced back into the house and told his wife, "It's going to be okay. Everything will be fine. You'll see. If that little cactus can make it here so can we." His wife looked at him as if he were a gallina sin cabeza but in the end his prediction turned out to be true. Though the Lopez family would never flourish in Espantosa, they did manage to survive. Barely. Throughout the years, the milagro nopal, as it came to be known, clung stubbornly to life, even after Hilario had died and his wife had lost her mind.

Guadalupe, now a woman of more than eighty years, stared down at the cactus sadly. They were the last of their line. They had come into the world together and now they seemed destined to go out the same way. Guadalupe shook her head and smacked her lips.

"It's a miracle we lasted this long," she said to the nopal. Then she turned and ambled slowly back to her house.

Melchor Mendoza watched the yellow dodge pull up in front of the Tumbleweed Café from the window of his second floor apartment. Melchor's view was unique in Espantosa. His apartment stood atop the old Rialto, the decrepit but still operational theater he'd inherited from his aunt, Maria Walsh, who was once the richest and most beautiful woman in Dimmit County. Melchor kept the theater running, but few customers ever came. Distributors had long ago ceased to send him films. The only film he had now was the last one he had been sent: *The French Connection*. Every now and then, someone came to see the show, usually teenagers looking for a private place to make out. In all of Espantosa, there was no place more private than The Rialto.

Melchor was thirty-five years old, less than average height, and stocky. He had a broad face, wide lips, and a nose that appeared too small for his face. He had coffee-colored eyes set too far apart and a full head of bushy black hair that was almost always uncombed. In the last election ever held in Espantosa, Mendoza had campaigned energetically, papering the town with fliers and canvassing the electorate over and over, and this despite the fact that he was running unopposed. Assured of victory, what Mendoza wanted was nothing less than a mandate from the people of Espantosa. On the morning of the election, he proudly cast his vote then retired to his campaign headquarters, the old realty office. In the end, Mendoza won by a single vote, his own. Though Mendoza was declared the winner, some in Espantosa question how he could be Mayor when he did not represent a clear majority. For a long time, it was a standing joke to refer to Mendoza as "your Honor." Mendoza would nod and smile. Over time, the joke wore thin, but the title stuck.

Melchor, lacking the mandate he'd dreamed of, did manage to enact several changes over the years. His initiatives included placing parking meters on Houston Street, purchasing uniforms for the volunteer fire department, and installing speed bumps in front of the high school. But undoubtedly his biggest success, and most disappointing failure, was luring an East Coast manufacturer of grommets to Espantosa.

The manufacturers had arrived in Espantosa in the middle of a hot August day. Dressed in business suits, they stepped out of their rental car and were immediately greeted by the Titan Marching Band, which that year consisted of three tubas, a trombone, and a cornet. Four cheerleaders rushed up to the industrialists and handed each of them a bouquet of wilted flowers, as Mendoza, dressed in a Hawaiian shirt and Bermuda shorts, grinned maniacally and pumped the hands of each of the men.

The industrialists were lured by low wages and Melchor's claim that the town boasted an abandoned plant that could easily be refitted to serve their purpose. This plant turned out to be an abandoned goat dairy. The manufacturers spent only an hour in town, carrying back with them nothing more than a couple of bad sunburns. Still, Mendoza dreamed of the day when he would put Espantosa on the map.

A brown-haired girl in loose trousers and a baggy shirt got out of the car and walked up to the café, a backpack over her shoulder. She tried the door, but it was locked. She then turned and scanned the street on both sides. Melchor could not see her face, but he had a sense that she was on the pretty side. He glanced at the clock. It was nearly ten, almost time for Sunday service. He turned from the window and slipped on his shoes.

A dark, narrow stair led from the apartment to the ground floor. At the bottom of the stairs Melchor opened the heavy door with the word "Private" printed in faded gold letters and walked across the dusty parquet floor.

Visitors were rare in Espantosa, except during deer season when camouflaged hunters in pickup trucks and SUVs invaded the town on weekends. It was not deer season, and even if it had been the arrival of an unaccompanied female would have attracted Melchor's attention. In a town of a little more than a thousand souls, available women were as rare as rose bushes, and most, like the American

Beauty in Herbie Menchaca's front yard, had lost their bloom long ago. Over the years, Melchor had developed a rich fantasy life, culminating in failed attempts at masturbation. He could never climax. At the final moment, he always had the same unsettling vision of himself projected onto the big screen, and the theater full of teenagers watching him and laughing. Now, as he unlocked the doors and looked up the street his mind flashed with the image of the girl and him together. He watched her undress shyly, exposing her breasts, the flesh of her thighs. He watched her lips part as he slowly approached her.

"Fine day, a good day, a grand morning!" a voice said behind him.

Melchor turned sharply. "Good morning, Pastor," he said. Pastor Gill was a tall man, nearly six-foot-three. He towered over Melchor, who often found himself looking up at the Pastor, an attitude which made him feel uncomfortably subordinate. He had acquired the habit when they spoke of not meeting the Pastor's eye, but rather gazing at a fixed point somewhere nearer to his own eye level. For his part, the Pastor, anxious to catch Melchor's attention, had the habit of bobbing around the smaller man like an anxious stork.

"Good morning, Mr. Mendoza. A fine day, a grand morning."

"Yes," Melchor agreed noncommittally.

"The flock will gather, Mr. Mendoza, and the Lord will smile."

Edward Gill was the head of the House on the Rock, a non-denominational church, as well as the owner and sole agent of Heavenly Acres

Real Estate Agency. The residents of Espantosa often confused these two enterprises. To make matters worse, the Pastor wore the same gold blazer in both occupations, and he often forgot to replace the decorative Frank Lloyd Wright nametag with the silver crucifix he wore on Sundays. Pastor Gill had intended to construct a suitable abode for the Church on the Rock, but funds were always lacking. For the past two years he held services in The Rialto.

"One of these days, Mr. Mendoza, I'm gonna come and see this show." Pastor Gill was standing in front of the faded poster advertising *The Graduate*.

"It's not showing anymore, Pastor," said Melchor.

"Really? I thought this was the one."

"No."

"Well, I'm gonna come some time, you wait and see."

Melchor reflected that Pastor Gill was one of the few people in Espantosa who hadn't seen *The French Connection*.

"Well," said the Pastor, "it's about that time." He went outside and stood on the broken steps, waiting for his flock, that consisted of no more than a couple of dozen souls any Sunday.

Melchor climbed up to the projection booth and settled down into the small sofa he kept there. When he was a child, he used to visit his aunt and she let him thread the enormous projector. He would often fall asleep to the rhythmic ticking of film passing over and under the metal gears.

Melchor's contribution to the service was limited to turning a tape machine on and off and adjusting the lighting on cues from the Pastor. Gill liked to achieve a dramatic effect by dimming the lights at the beginning, and raising the level of illumination gradually. Melchor considered it a cheap effect, but obliged because the Pastor paid $100 a month to rent the theater.

Melchor piped in the music as the flock began to gather. Recently, the Pastor had shown signs of loosening up where the music was concerned. The traditional Tennessee Ernie Ford and Jim Nabors had been replaced by Christian Rock and the occasional pop tune. Before the service, Gill handed Melchor a cassette. "I think you're gonna like this selection, Mr. Mendoza," he said with a wink. As the music rose, Melchor was surprised to hear Johnny Lee singing "Looking for Love in All the Wrong Places."

"The other day, I was stopped in the street by a lonely man," the pastor said. His voice was low and intimate in the near darkness. "He asked me where can a man find a good time? Do you know what I told him? Friends, I told him if all he wanted was a good time, there were better places to live than Espantosa." A few snickers from the flock. "No, seriously, friends, I said to him that 'a good time' meant different things to different people." Melchor raised the lights almost imperceptibly. "For one man, a good time is sitting on the banks of a river, watching his cork bobble on the waves. For another man, a good time is standing at a bar sipping whiskey or gin." Melchor raised the lights again. "But for me, a good time was being in my own home with my wife, reading from the

9

Good Book." The lights grew stronger. "That lonely man told me then that he didn't have a family. Friends, I smiled. We are all members of the same family, I said to him, and he looked at me strangely." Melchor raised the lights again. "Yes, my friends, I told him we are all part of the same, loving family, and I took him in my arms." Melchor turned the lights up all the way. "And that lonely man, who no one'd touched for so many years, who wandered through life as a man in a hopeless desert, he wept, friends, he wept in my arms, and I wept also." The pastor leaned back and raised his arms to the ceiling. "Friends, we are all fellow travelers..."

Melchor had stopped listening. He had noticed that the girl he saw across the street was sitting in the theater. She appeared to be writing something in a notebook she held on her lap. Melchor left the booth and walked down to the theater. He slipped silently into a seat several rows behind her and to the left. From this vantage point, he could see her profile, and he could already tell that she was not pretty. She had a snub nose and a weak chin. It was impossible to tell if she was fat or slim. Her clothes fitted her like a loose sack.

"For the first shall be last," said Gill, "and all manner of being shall be well. Let him who is without a stone cast his glance toward Heaven..."

Melchor looked up at the Pastor who had fallen to his knees. The flock was also on their knees in the narrow space between the seats, hands raised toward the ceiling. "And lead us not into temptation, and lead us not into temptation, temptation, temptation..."

When the service was over, the girl remained in her seat. The flock gathered around the Pastor who wiped the sweat from his brow with a white handkerchief. Melchor continued to watch the girl. She was writing in her notebook, her head down. He thought this made her look like a schoolgirl.

As the flock began to head toward the doors, the girl got up and looked around. She spotted Melchor and approached him.

"Do you work here?" she asked. It was almost an accusation.

"Yes," said Melchor.

"Who owns this place?"

"I do."

"Can you tell me when this theater was constructed?"

"In nineteen-fifty-four. It was built by..."

"And has it been in continuous operation?" the girl interrupted.

"There's always been a movie showing, if that's what you're asking."

The girl looked around the theater. "What's showing?" she asked.

"The movie? *The French Connection*."

"I've seen that movie."

"I hear that a lot," Melchor grinned. "What's all this about? You writing a guidebook or something?"

"Yes."

"You're joking." But he could see she was not.

"I passed one gas station on the way in. Is that the only one?"

"There's the Pak-n-Sip on the highway," he said.

"I see." She scribbled some more.

Melchor cleared his throat. "You staying long?"

"Just as long as it takes."

"The last motel we had closed ten years ago."

"No accommodations," she said, making another note.

Pastor Gill approached the girl. "Mr. Mendoza, may I introduce myself?" he said, smiling broadly. "My name is Gill," he said to the girl. "I'm the pastor of this church. We are always pleased to have a stranger attend our services. Whereabouts do you come from?"

The girl looked back at him coldly and did not accept the hand he offered. "I'm an atheist," she said.

Gill smiled. He was on familiar ground. "The Lord believes in you, sister, even if you don't believe in the Lord. Why don't you come round to my house and we can argue about it over coffee and cake."

"Fuck off," she said, glaring at him.

At that moment, Pastor Gill's wife arrived. She stood a few feet behind her husband, her arms across her ample belly. Her upper lip was moist, and the small tip of her pink tongue could be seen between her white teeth. She cleared her throat.

The Pastor said nothing, so the introductions fell to Melchor. "Mrs. Gill, this is..." He paused. The girl glared at him insolently. "This is Miss..." he tried again.

Mrs. Gill, with the social grace acquired from years of watching *Masterpiece Theater*, extended her small, pudgy hand. "How do you do?" she said.

The girl stared at her. Mrs. Gill withdrew her hand with a smile. "My dear," she said. "You have such lovely eyes! I would die for those eyebrows." She took the girl by the elbow and said, "Come over here and tell me your story. I'm sure you lead a very adventurous life. I want to know all about you." The girl seemed unsure of how to thwart the assault. She allowed herself to be led away.

Melchor and Pastor Gill watched the two women sitting together talking in quiet tones.

"No good will come of this," said Pastor Gill.

Chapter Two

Over the next several days, the girl was the object of much curiosity. The Tumbleweed Café was abuzz with gossip.

"Where's she staying?" asked Fent Hurley. He was a farmer and only came into town once a week so he was not fully abreast of current events.

"She's holed up in the Pastor's house," said Roy Blas, plating up a burger and fries and slapping his hand down on the brass bell he'd recently installed on the counter.

Connie Mays looked over at Roy and scowled. She was standing not three feet from the counter. The bell, she felt, was quite unnecessary and it annoyed her. She picked up the plate and sniffed her disapproval.

Connie was thirty-four years old and had been working at the Tumbleweed Café for nearly five years, ever since returning to Espantosa to care for her aging mother. She had soft blue eyes, brown hair, and full lips. She was the kind of woman you could pass in the street day after day and never notice, until suddenly, for some unknown reason, she would make you stop and stare.

"What's that girl doing here anyway?" asked Hurley.

"Writing a guidebook according to Your Honor," said Roy.

"A guidebook? You don't say?"

"It's true," said Roy proudly. "We're gonna be in the book."

"What's her name?" asked Hurley.

"Amanda," said Gorman. "Amanda Coakely. She's an atheist."

"Well, I'll be," said Hurley. He stared down into his coffee cup and shook his head.

"And she sleeps naked," Gorman added. Gorman ran a septic tank service and was a notorious peeping tom. His pronouncement was treated with some respect.

"Naked?"

"As the day she was born," said Gorman, smiling to reveal his yellow teeth.

The Book, as residents of Espantosa came to call it, caused an even greater sensation than the girl herself. Everyone wanted to be sure they made it into The Book, and there was fierce competition among the residents over who could grab the most ink in the guide.

When the yellow Dodge pulled into French's Fill Up Station, the owner, Bill French, insisted on filling the tank himself.

"The sign says self-service," Miss Coakely observed.

"Well, technically speaking, we are no longer a full-service filling station, but we do offer a personal touch for special customers."

"I don't want special treatment."

"No, of course not," French protested. "What I mean to say is, we consider everyone a special customer."

"If everyone is special, then no one is special," said Miss Coakely. She reached into the front seat of the car and took out her notebook.

French looked at the book and licked his lips. "I guess I never thought of it that way. I can see you're right. Anyway, that's how we operate."

15

"When was this station constructed?" asked Miss Coakely.

"Nineteen-fifty-seven. It was built by..." French stared aghast as Miss Coakely noted the date and closed the book. "I could tell you some stories," he said quickly, grabbing a squeegee and beginning to wash the windows.

Miss Coakely, about to put the book back into the car, paused and looked at him dubiously.

"Once, Steve McQueen came through here. I filled up his tank for him. He was polite, but a lousy tipper." Miss Coakely started to put the book back again and French hastily added, "He had a whole film crew with him. Seems they were making a movie."

Miss Coakely opened the book. "Do you know the name of the movie?"

"Let me see," said French, leaning on the hood of the car. "It was the one about that big chase. He was on the run from the law. What was the name of that movie?"

"*The Getaway*?" Miss Coakely offered.

"That's the one! Yup. Came right through Espantosa, making a movie." French grinned as he watched the girl making notes.

"How long was the crew in town?" she asked.

"How long?" French wiped his forehead with a greasy red towel. "Well, not long. I don't think they were here more than a day."

"I see," said the girl, scribbling.

French leaned closer and whispered to the girl, "Rumor has it, he was caught by the sheriff with some, um, contraband."

Miss Coakely looked up from her notebook. "Drugs?"

"Yup. He was busted right here in Espantosa. Spent a night in jail."

"I thought you said they only remained a day?"

"Well, yeah, a day, counting the night. From one afternoon to the next morning, if you take my meaning. 'Course the press hushed it up."

"What press?"

"There was a reporter with 'em. He kept it quiet. In fact," French added, "I don't know too many people ever even knew they was in town."

If this point stretched the story beyond credulity, Miss Coakely did not appear to notice. She reached into her pocket to pay.

"No, no," said French. "No charge. We're honored to have you, Miss Coakely, honored to have you."

"I don't accept gratuities," said Miss Coakely primly.

"It's not a gratuity. It's a gift. Anyhow, I insist."

The girl shrugged. She got into her car and started it.

"Now, Miss Coakely," French added, "I wouldn't go 'round asking folk about the story I told you. Most people swore to secrecy, outta respect."

Miss Coakely shrugged.

Mr. French watched the car pull away and whistled under his breath. "Bill French," he said to himself, "You're an awful good liar, an awful good liar."

Mr. French was not alone in possessing this talent. Upon visiting the post office, Miss Coakely learned that the postmaster was a war veteran and had saved the life of Audie Murphy, and that Louise Schneider, who happened to be buying stamps, had a great aunt who had survived the Titanic. Indeed, if Miss Coakely had been researching a novel, she could not have found a richer source of fiction than among the citizens of Espantosa.

Miss Coakely duly noted everything she was told. Some of the stories she heard began to take on a life of their own. Once word got around that Bill French had spun a tale about Steve McQueen, other residents began to recount their own adventures with the movie star. Judging by the number of stories she heard, Miss Coakely calculated that the star spent far longer than a single day in Espantosa. By the end of the week, it was general knowledge he'd stayed a full month and shot several scenes in the movie at various locations around the town. Sadly, residents informed her, much of what was filmed wound up on the cutting room floor.

"He and his girlfriend sat right here and ate a meal together. They were so much in love, you could just tell," said Roy. He took out a menu and showed Miss Coakely an entry that read, 'Lovers Special.' "That's what they had. A big meal. I wonder how she kept her figure, that girl, eating so much every day." Roy had carefully written out the menu the night before.

Though Miss Coakely stated she did not accept gifts, the people of Espantosa continued to offer her goods and services at no charge. She always protested but usually took what was offered. She never uttered a word of thanks and on many occasions was outright rude. The residents were willing to overlook her faults for the sake of the town.

Since the girl's arrival, Melchor had watched her come and go from his apartment window. She had not returned to the Rialto, apparently having learned all she needed to know on her one brief visit. When he ran into Pastor Gill at the hardware store, he asked how things were going. The Pastor rolled his eyes.

"She's a tough little nut," he said. "And I'll tell you what, I wouldn't let a daughter of mine roam around the country on her own like that. Her parents oughta have more sense. Just asking for trouble, she is."

"What kind of trouble?" said Melchor.

"There's evil in the world, Mr. Mendoza," he said, shaking his head. He leaned closer and whispered, "You know she sleeps naked?"

Melchor flushed. "Really?" he said.

"No good will come of it," Pastor Gill repeated. "No good at *all*."

Melchor left the hardware store and walked quickly across the street to the theater. He walked up the stairs, feeling his penis stiffening against his leg. He entered his apartment and threw himself on the bed, fumbling with his trousers. He closed his eyes and tried to picture the girl naked on her back. He imagined himself standing in her room. She was asleep and he stood beside the bed, slowly stroking himself. Her lips parted and she moaned softly. He began to stroke himself more quickly. His heart began to pound. His breath quickened. He

19

could feel the blood rushing to his head, his ears burning.

Then, suddenly, the image of the girl vanished. He was standing in the middle of an abandoned warehouse. He was naked, with his penis in his hand and Gene Hackman was standing across from him.

"What the fuck?" said Hackman.

Melchor stared down at his body, enormous, flat, stretched out across the faded silver screen. He looked over the rows of seats. They were filled with laughing teenagers, Pastor Gill and Mrs. Gill, and in the front row, the girl, scribbling in her notebook.

Melchor sat bolt upright in bed. He brushed the sweat from his brow and pulled up his trousers. His attempt at masturbation left him feeling frustrated and morose. He got up and paced the room briefly, then sat down at the flimsy desk beside the window, picked up a pen and began to write.

Over the years, Melchor had written many letters such as the one he was writing now. One drawer of the tiny desk was filled with them. None had ever been mailed.

Due to the recent discovery of the historic nature of the Rialto... the famed Rialto, it seems clear that your company might be... would be wise to consider once again distributing films to this theater... this historic theater, recently featured in a guidebook for our region. It is believed that the Rialto is the last theater of its kind operating in this part of the country.

Melchor paused. He realized it would be helpful to have a quote from the Book here. But what had Miss Coakely written? No one, so far as he knew, had seen a single word.

He looked out the window and noted the battered yellow Dodge was parked outside the Post Office.

Melchor went downstairs and crossed the street quickly. He reached the Post Office just as the girl was emerging.

"Hello, Miss Coakely," he said. "I was wondering how the Book is coming?"

The girl turned up the street and Melchor followed. "Fine," she said, tucking her notebook into her backpack.

"Well, I was wondering...." She turned to look at him and he could sense her body poised for rejection. "I wondered if," Melchor pressed forward, "I could ask to see what you wrote about the Rialto?"

Miss Coakely seemed relieved. Melchor realized that she probably thought he was going to ask her out. "That's confidential. You'll see it when it comes out."

"It's just that I'm trying to get the distributors to start sending movies again, you see. It would help a lot if I had a quote from the book."

"I don't see how that would help," She had an ungainly walk, as if one of her legs might be shorter than the other. Melchor had to slow down to keep from leaving her behind.

"I just thought something about the historic nature of the theater, describing it as a landmark or something."

"Are you trying to tell me what to write?"

"No, no," Melchor could feel the opportunity slipping away. "It's just that if you *did* write that, it would help me a lot."

"I can't talk about what I write."

"I understand. Maybe if you could just, kind of privately, not for the book, so to speak, give me a few sentences about what you think of the Rialto, then I could..."

"I don't think that would help."

"No, it would be great."

The girl stopped suddenly. "Look, do you want to know what I think of your theater? I think it's a joke. There's nothing historical about it. It should have been demolished years ago. I can't imagine why you keep showing the same Goddamn movie night after night, year after year, except you're too pathetic to actually do something with your life. Now, if that's what you want me to write down for you, I'll be happy to do that, otherwise, leave me the fuck alone!"

Melchor stared at her dumbfounded. She gave him a smoldering look, then raised her hand. For a moment, he thought she was going to strike him. He retreated a step. She brought her hand down in a quick chopping motion and screamed, "Fuck you!" Then she turned and walked quickly away. He stared at her back, sensing the anger pulsing through her body.

He walked slowly back to the Rialto, climbed the stairs, and entered the apartment. He picked up the letter, scanned it briefly, and threw it into the trash.

Chapter Three

"I hear she told Melchor off yesterday. He asked what was in the Book."

"She told him to fuck off, loud as thunder," said Roy. "I heard it all the way back in the kitchen. That girl has a mouth on her."

"You're right about that," Connie agreed. "Can't imagine how the Pastor puts up with her."

"Well, he's whipped, that's plain," said Gorman. "Mrs. Gill has taken that girl under her wing like a fat mother hen."

"Melchor wanted her to write something good about the Rialto. Seems he's trying to get the movie folk to send him another show," said Mrs. Nelson, who ran the hardware store with her son, Bruce.

"Wanted her to declare it a historical landmark," Bruce said.

"I'm beginning to wonder what she's saying myself," said Connie. "Nobody's seen a word she's written in that notebook of hers. She scribbles and scribbles, but what does she say?"

"What's there to say?" Gorman asked. "It's a piece of shit town, we all know that."

"I don't see what's so bad about Espantosa," said Mrs. Nelson. "Lotsa places is worse than here."

"Name one," said Gorman. A glum silence followed in which the only sound was the sizzle of bacon on the grill in the kitchen. "Yup. That about sums it up."

"Mr. Gill and I always take our coffee on the porch," said Mrs. Gill, cleaning up the plates from dinner. "I hope you'll make it a habit to join us while you're staying here."

Miss Coakely rose. "I've had a long day. I think I'll go to bed now."

"It's so early," said Mrs. Gill.

The Pastor leaned back in his chair. "Perhaps Miss Coakely doesn't care for our company," he said.

"Don't be rude, Edward," his wife scolded. "I'm sure nothing could be further from the truth. She's just tired, I expect."

"Yes," Miss Coakely agreed.

"You run along, dear. I think it's so rare to find a young person who keeps decent hours. It's a virtue, I'm *sure*. Don't you agree, Edward?"

The Pastor huffed and rose from the table. "I'll be on the porch," he said.

Miss Coakely said goodnight to Mrs. Gill and went to her room. It was a small, tidy space, with a narrow bed on a steel frame, a dresser, a nightstand, and an overstuffed chair. There was no lamp, and the light bulb was so bright that Miss Coakely preferred to turn it off and read by what little light seeped in through the branches of the overgrown oleander that grew outside the window. It was stuffy at night, and for this reason, Miss Coakely slept in the nude, on top of the sheets.

She undressed quickly, laying her clothes across the chair. She reached into her pocket and took out a small wad of bills and counted it. Eighteen dollars. She considered how far she could expect to get on eighteen dollars worth of gas. She had not spent a single dollar since coming to Espantosa, but she could hardly expect to earn much money while staying there. She was stuck, she realized, and sooner or later, she was going to have to start paying her own way.

She climbed onto the bed and lay flat on her back, staring up at the damp-stained ceiling. "God, what a shithole," she murmured.

A few hours later, she woke. The room was hot and humid. She felt the sheets sticking to her back. She rolled over and reached for the glass of water she'd left on the nightstand. As she turned, she froze. She stared at the door. It was no longer shut. She heard the floorboards creak in the hall and sprang out of bed. She flung open the door. At the other end of the hall, she saw the door to the Pastor's bedroom slowly close.

"Fuckin' pervert!" she yelled.

She went into the dining room and dragged a chair noisily through the hall, slammed the door and braced the chair against it.

Leroy Polk was sitting on a full bladder. He had four cups of coffee at the Tumbleweed Cafe that morning, which was not wise for a forty-two year old man with an enlarged prostate, especially one who, as Fent Hurley put it, sat around on his brains all day. Polk had been a Deputy Sheriff in Dimmitt County for almost twenty years. He was unmarried, and, since his girlfriend Belinda left two weeks ago, uninvolved. Polk told himself he was better off, but the event had shaken him badly. Never known for having a good disposition, Polk went about his duties with all the friendliness of a rattlesnake.

Now, as he eased his patrol car onto the main drag, he considered morosely where he was going to pee, an act that for Polk resembled trying to squeeze water out of a dry sponge.

When he spotted the yellow Dodge turning down the street, he smiled grimly and pulled up behind. He flashed his lights.

The driver of the car pulled over and the deputy got out of the car, approaching his prey with a swagger, one hand on his holster.

"May I see your license, Ma'am?" he said.

As Miss Coakely rummaged through her backpack, Polk reached into the open window and switched off the ignition. She glared at him. He took the license from her and opened his citation book. "Are you aware that you failed to signal for a turn?"

"There was no traffic."

"The law's the law, traffic or no."

"That's a stupid law," Miss Coakely protested.

"I don't write the laws, Ma'am," the Deputy said in his best Western drawl, "I just enforce 'em. You'll have to pay the fine or appear in court if you want to dispute the violation."

"You're damned right I dispute it," said Miss Coakely fiercely.

Polk tore out the citation and handed it to Miss Coakely. She crumpled up the ticket and tossed it onto the floor of her car.

"If you choose not to pay the fine, and you fail to appear in court, you can be jailed.

Perhaps you'd like to write about that in your little black book."

Miss Coakely glared at the sheriff, started her car, and pulled away from the curb. Polk watched her go and shook his head.

Melchor Mendoza was unimpressed by the tales being spun all over Espantosa. Stopping in for lunch at the Tumbleweed, he winced at the recent changes to the menu. When Connie came by to take his order, he pointed at the photo of Steve McQueen on a motorcycle next to a new item called the "Getaway Hoagie."

"Isn't this picture from *The Great Escape*?"

Connie laughed.

"What is it?"

"Bologna, lettuce and tomato, American cheese on a Kaiser roll," said Connie, rolling her eyes. "You sure you don't want one? Legend has it, Mr. McQueen ordered these special and ate four in one sitting."

"Was that before or after he consumed the Lover's Special?"

Roy, peering out of the kitchen, laid a plate on the counter and slapped the bell. Connie glanced over her shoulder and then leaned toward Melchor and whispered, "I'm about to stick that bell..."

"I'll just have a hamburger and fries," said Melchor, handing the menu to Connie. He grabbed a copy of *The Dimmitt County Caller* from the next table and began to leaf through it. As usual, there was no mention of Espantosa. It had been many years since the town had had its own paper, a painful issue for Melchor because the publisher, Umberto Marconi, had entrusted the *Espantosa Hourly Gazette* to him when he was forced by old age and ill health to retire to a nursing home in Carrizo Springs. Melchor had attempted to keep the paper going, but his heart was not in it. Besides, he was a terrible newspaperman, as Umberto never tired of pointing out. It was one more office, like Mayor, that Mendoza could add to his ragged résumé.

Connie brought over his drink and Melchor folded the paper and commented, "It's like we don't even exist."

"Maybe we don't," said Connie. She reached down and pinched Melchor's arm. "Well, you seem real enough anyway." Melchor grinned sheepishly. The truth is, he had always had a thing for Connie. It wasn't so much the way she looked, though Melchor considered her pretty. No, it was something else, something he found hard to define. Or maybe it was simply the fact that Connie actually seemed to flirt with him.

At that moment, the café door swung open and Miss Coakely entered.

"Of course we exist," Connie said sweetly. "That girl's gonna tell the whole world all about us."

Melchor nodded glumly. "Lot of good that'll do. Half the things she knows are outright lies."

"It's a pity there isn't anyone around to really represent the town," she said, walking away. "You know," she added over her shoulder, "like a Mayor, or something."

The remark stung Melchor. She was right. Even though he chafed at the wild fictions people had been spinning for the past several days, he realized he'd been no better. He took a deep breath and walked over to Miss Coakely's table.

"Do you mind if I sit down?" he asked.

Miss Coakely glared at him. "The sheriff in this town is a Gestapo," she said. "He gave me a fucking ticket."

"Leroy Polk?" Melchor slid into the seat opposite her. "He's not so bad. Just a little out of sorts these days. His girlfriend left him a couple of weeks ago."

"Gee, I wonder why."

Melchor laughed. "Takes all kinds, I guess. Maybe I can do something about your ticket." Miss Coakely looked at him dubiously. "I don't know if I mentioned that I'm sort of the Mayor."

"I was told Espantosa didn't have a Mayor," Miss Coakely said.

"Well, it's a long story. Anyway, I can talk to Leroy."

"Thanks," Miss Coakely mumbled.

"I was thinking that maybe I could help you out with your project, provide you with some historical perspective."

Miss Coakely shrugged.

"Have you been out to the lake, yet? It's something to see at night. Espantosa means fearful or frightening in Spanish, and it can be. A lot of legends surround that lake, dating all the way back to when it was a stopover on the Camino Real. That's the colonial highway used by the Spaniards," Melchor explained. "John King Fisher and his band were active in these parts. A lot of gold went missing and a lot of people lost their lives."

Melchor leaned closer and lowered his voice. "There are stories people tell about giant

Lechuzas, or owls, that haunt the banks. They're ghostly creatures, unnatural." Melchor manufactured a shiver for effect.

Miss Coakely scowled. "I've heard all about it. I'm writing a guidebook, not a book of horror stories."

"Well," said Melchor, leaning back, "it's just local color, I guess."

Connie brought their food. She gave Melchor a wink of encouragement.

"Anyway, the town's been here for more than a hundred years. Of course, it wasn't always like this. It really took off for a time back in the fifties. This guy from Australia arrived, said he wanted to raise goats. He told people everyone would be drinking goat milk instead of cow milk in a few years time. I don't think anyone believed him, but they sure were happy to take his money."

"Sounds like a stupid idea," said Miss Coakely, slurping her coke.

"I agree, I agree. Still, things went pretty well for some time. There was work to do, building the dairy, minding the goats, trucking the milk to God knows where. He had nearly a hundred workers at one time. At the peak, he had almost ten thousand goats. Then there was a blight of some sort, killed off some of the goats. They had to put the rest down. They burned the carcasses. People say he wept like a baby when they did that."

"Like I said, it sounds like a stupid idea."

"I know," Melchor admitted. "Anyway, by the time he left, a lot of the workers had a foothold here and for a while the town continued to grow. Then the real blight came. They opened the interstate and everything, I mean everything, just about died."

"I see."

"So you're looking at a town that's frankly seen better days, and will again, I believe."

Connie arrived to fill Mendoza's cup. The girl asked for her check.

"Never you mind," said Roy, from behind the counter. "You just think of our café as your home away from home. Your money's no good with us."

Miss Coakely rose to leave.

"I was wondering," said Melchor, rising and following her to the door, "if maybe we could sit down together and talk about your book. Maybe I could help you out. Guide you around the town."

Miss Coakely gave him a sharp look. "I can't discuss the book with anyone."

"I understand," said Melchor. "It's just that I think Espantosa has a lot to offer, even though it's not easy to see. On the surface, I mean."

"Such as what?"

"Well..." Melchor faltered. He looked back helplessly over his shoulder at Connie. "There's always, um, the yearly festival."

"Festival?"

"Absolutely. One of the best. You have to stay for that."

"I'm on a schedule."

"It's in two weeks," said Melchor. "It's something to write about, I promise you."

Miss Coakely hoisted her backpack onto her shoulder. "We'll see," she said, turning to leave. "I can't make any promises."

Connie waited until Miss Coakely disappeared, then rushed up to Melchor and grabbed him by the arm. "What the hell were you talking about? Just what kind of festival is this?"

Melchor smiled nervously. "I'll let you know," he answered. "Just as soon as I figure it out myself."

Chapter Four

Though Guadalupe Lopez had brought more than a hundred children into the world, she had never had any of her own. She had been married once, when she was in her early twenties, but her husband died or ran off with another woman, depending on what story she felt like telling.

As a girl she had been wild, running through the streets of Espantosa like a gallina sin cabeza. She was famous for eating dirt and making pets of unusual creatures (possums, frogs, even a polecat). After the death of her father, her mother never left the house except at night when she would wander through the streets wailing like la llorona.

When Guadalupe's mother died, it was several weeks before the body was discovered. Neighbors noticed a foul smell and investigated. What they saw when they kicked down the door took their breath away. There was decaying food everywhere, and piles of feces in the corners of every room. When they opened the door to the bedroom, they got another shock. The body was on the bed and badly decomposed. Piled around the bed were hundreds of pairs of men's shoes.

The missing shoes had long been a mystery in Espantosa. Nearly every man in town had lost several pairs, and until then no one had been able to explain their disappearance.

"Those are my workboots," said Hector Mendoza, Melchor's grandfather. "Jesus."

They found Guadalupe huddled in a closet, clutching a ragged doll. She was filthy and looked up at them like a feral animal.

Guadalupe was taken in by her great aunt, Hortencia, who tamed the girl and, it was rumored, taught her the ways of the curandera. Though she would never learn to read or write, Guadalupe would come to have an encyclopedic knowledge of local horticulture. She assisted her aunt in delivering babies and eventually took over the job completely.

It was Hortencia who first taught Guadalupe the secret of transforming her heart so that it beat like a rabbit's or fluttered in her chest like that of a hummingbird. In time, she learned what it was to soar in the sky like a hawk or burrow in the blind, dark earth like a worm. Through Hortencia, Guadalupe discovered the animal within her.

It was during this time that the legend of La Lechuza was born. People claimed to have seen an enormous owl flying over the darkened waters of the Espantosa on moonless nights. Some said its wings spanned more than six feet and that anyone who heard its call would suffer some misfortune.

When her great aunt died, Guadalupe moved back into her mother's house. Though her wild days were behind her, she continued to inspire all kinds of stories, and was almost as popular a bedtime threat as Sammy the Smiling Goat Chupacabra. Most of the townspeople treated Guadalupe with a mixture of fear and respect.

Without a doubt Guadalupe's most famous deed was the time she put the evil eye on Howard Meeks, the county Tax Assessor.

Meeks had only been on the job for a week when he learned that Guadalupe's house was in arrears and had been so for a ridiculously long time.

"You mean no one has collected taxes on that house in eighteen years?" Meeks asked his assistant Henry Arispe.

"It's not that easy," Henry explained. "The owner is a crazy woman named Guadalupe Lopez. People say she's a curandera. A witch." Meeks rolled his eyes. Henry continued. "Getting her outta that house is no easy matter."

"Serve her with papers," said Meeks.

"Been done."

"Listen," said Meeks, growing impatient, "that house belongs to the county. Have the constable evict her and put a lock on it."

"Also been done."

"And?"

"She just breaks the lock and goes back inside."

"Christ!"

"The problem is, it's our house. The county's, I mean. But it's not like we can actually do anything with it. It would never sell."

"Why not?"

Henry lit a cigarette as Meeks frowned. It was one of Henry's habits, like extended lunches, that Meeks meant to change, and soon.

"You been there yet?" Henry asked, blowing smoke in the general direction of his boss. "Well, *when* you go there, you'll see."

The next day Meeks went to Espantosa. He pulled up at Bill French's gas station in his car with the Tax Assessor insignia on the door panel. French took one look at the logo and began to sweat.

"I'm looking for Cerralvo Street," he told French.

Like most people in Espantosa, Bill French was behind in his taxes, so he was understandably relieved when he discovered the assessor was not coming to see *him*. On the other hand, he couldn't help feeling sorry for the poor son-of-a-bitch who was in trouble.

"Cevallo Street?" said French scratching his chin.

"Cerralvo," Meeks corrected him.

"Never heard of it."

Meeks looked at him over the top of his glasses. "What? You can't tell me in a town this size..."

"Hell, boss, half the streets around here got no signs. You might have a name on a map..."

"But how do you get around then?"

French laughed softly, sizing up his customer quickly and dismissing him as a college-educated idiot. "Well, let's see," he drawled. "I guess we get around 'cause we lived here all our lives."

Meeks sighed. "I'm looking for a woman named Guadalupe Lopez. Her house."

"Why didn't you say so in the first place?" French proceeded to give the assessor directions while Meeks listened patiently. "And don't forget," he added as Meeks climbed back into his car, "if you pass the water tower, you've gone too far."

"The water tower," Meeks nodded.

As soon as the tax assessor pulled away French went inside and phoned Dottie Price. Guadalupe didn't have a phone, but Dottie lived just down the street.

"Dottie," he said, "there's a tax assessor in town." Dottie gasped and almost dropped the phone. "Now settle down. He's after Guadalupe. You better send someone over there to warn her. I sent him on a wild goose chase. With any luck he's already lost."

Meeks *was* lost. He had been driving for a quarter of an hour and had not even managed to find the water tower, which would have at least given him a point of reference. Driving slowly down the road in his Crown Victoria, he spotted a teenage boy and pulled over. He motioned the boy to his car.

"You know where Guadalupe Lopez lives?" he asked.

"Que?" said the boy, leaning in the car window and enjoying the blast of cool air.

"Do you speak English?"

"Si," said the boy, grinning.

"Can you tell me where the water tower is?"

"Que?"

"Dammit," said Meeks. He rolled up his window and pulled away.

"Dumbass," said the boy. At that moment his mother poked her head out of the screen door and asked who was in that big shiny car.

"Just some pendejo. He's looking for the water tower," the boy grinned.

"We don't have a water tower," said the boy's mother.

"Like I said, he's a pendejo."

Meeks drove around Espantosa for the better part of an hour. He would never have imagined it would be so hard to find one house in such a small town. The problem was that Espantosa was spread out over a fairly large area, with long expanses of unused land between clusters of houses. Also, the map he had was hopelessly out of date. Streets that were indicated on the map no longer existed and streets that did exist were not on the map.

In desperation, he pulled next to a ramshackle row of houses and asked a barefooted ten year old girl who was playing marbles with bottle caps in her sandy front yard if she knew where he could find Guadalupe Lopez. The girl looked up at him and pointed to the house next door.

The Tax Assessor looked over at the house and gasped. He knew now what Henry meant. The house was in terrible condition, with missing shingles on the roof and a lopsided porch that looked like it might topple in the slightest breeze. One window was covered with plywood and holes in the siding had been patched with two-by-fours.

"This is not a house," Meeks muttered, "it's an accident waiting to happen."

He walked up the gravel path and nearly turned his ankle on a pothole the size of a dinner plate. He stepped gingerly onto the porch, feeling the wood sag beneath his weight. He knocked on the front door.

There was no answer. He knocked again. Then he tried the doorknob, but it was locked. He reached into his briefcase and took out some tools and began to work the lock. Unlike the rest of the house, the lock proved surprisingly sound. Finally, he put a large screwdriver against the doorjamb and began to chip away at it. Then the door opened.

"What the hell are you doing?" The woman in the doorway was an imposing figure. She was tall and heavy, with beefy forearms that would have been the envy of any sailor. Her hair was a wild tangle of black and gray curls. She had an enormous mole on the left side of her face from which sprouted three long, black hairs. "This is my house!" she shouted.

Meeks, a tall, slight man, recoiled involuntarily. Collecting himself he stammered, "No, no, this house belongs to the county."

"The hell you say! Get out of here you cabrón pig before I break your scrawny neck."

"Madam..."

"What's that?" Guadalupe moved forward menacingly. "What did you call me? You think I'm a whore?"

"Er, Miss, you cannot threaten a county official. I have the authority..."

"You don't have shit. Now get off my porch before I get my shotgun."

Meeks, who had been cowering unawares, straightened up and squared his puny shoulders. "All right, but I'll be back."

"You better bring an army with you, you son-of-a-bitch!"

Meeks collected his tools and turned to leave. He was surprised to see the entire scene had been played out before an audience of Guadalupe's neighbors and other interested parties. Even Bill French was there, leaning on the front of his pickup. He'd closed the shop just for the occasion. The spectators applauded and cheered as the Tax Assessor walked back to his big shiny Crown Victoria with the county insignia on the door panel.

When he got back to the office, Henry was sitting in front of a file cabinet smoking a cigarette and dropping ash onto the records.

"Put that cigarette out!" Meeks bellowed.

Henry complied, dropping his cigarette into a Coke can. "How'd it go?"

"That house," said Meeks through clenched teeth, "belongs to the county."

"Sure," Henry said agreeably. And as he watched his boss walk into his office and slam the door, he added under the breath, "But what are we gonna do with it?"

The next day, Meeks woke up with a hacking cough. He went to work but by noon it was clear he was in no condition to be there.

"Get on the phone to the constable and have him serve papers on that woman," he told Henry between coughs.

"Sure," said Henry, "but I told you, it's been done."

"We're gonna do it again." Meeks wiped his mouth with a handkerchief. He looked down at it and gasped. It was black.

Meeks did not go to work the next day, or the day after. He spent most of his time in bed, sweating and shivering and coughing out his lungs. On the third day of his illness he woke up in the middle of the night and was shaken by a coughing fit so intense he almost passed out. By this time, he felt like he had swallowed a box of needles every time he took a breath. The next morning he slowly and painfully dressed and drove himself down to the doctor's office.

The doctor, a young kid just out of medical school, examined Meeks carefully. He asked his patient to breathe deeply as he listened to his chest, but this prompted a coughing fit so intense the doctor feared he might lose him on the spot. When the fit finally subsided, Meeks wiped his mouth with a kleenex and showed it to the physician. It was stained with a dark, sticky mucus.

"Give me a minute," said the young medico. "Try to relax."

A few minutes later, the doctor returned. Meeks looked up at him weakly. "Mr. Meeks have you ever worked in or around a coal mine?" he asked.

"What... the... hell?" Meeks whispered hoarsely.

"Well, the thing is, as near as I can figure, and I'm no expert on this condition..."

Meeks waved his hand limply. "Just... give it... to me... straight."

"All right. Near as I can figure, you're suffering from all the symptoms of black lung disease. Only thing is, I can't figure how you ever contracted it in the middle of South Texas."

When word got around Espantosa what had happened to the Tax Assessor, people shook their heads and muttered, not without sympathy, "She's put a hex on that poor bastard." Their sympathy did not, however, prevent many locals from starting a pool betting on just when the Assessor would kick the bucket.

When Henry learned of his boss's condition, he told his wife, "That old witch has put a hex on the dumb bastard."

His wife, Tina, who was standing at the sink snapping the ends off a colander of Kentucky Wonder Beans, said over her shoulder, "Well, you told that pendejo shithead not to go around bothering that woman. He should have listened to you." Tina harbored the conviction, not unfounded, that her husband was worth ten of his boss. When the position came open, she had insisted Henry interview for it, though he protested it was a waste of time.

"No Mexican is ever gonna be made Tax Assessor in this county," he explained.

That he had been proved right did little to appease his wife's anger over his lack of ambition.

Now, as he looked at her from behind, admiring her slim shoulders, the beauty of her ass, Henry got up from the table and kissed the back of her neck, whispering soft indecencies into her ear.

Tina leaned back and sighed and he reached around and cupped her breasts.

"Men!" said Tina, tossing a Wonder Bean at her husband over her shoulder.

A half hour later, as they lay in bed together after making love, Henry lit a cigarette and said to his wife, "Just the same, I better see what I can do to help the poor bastard."

The next morning, Henry drove to Espantosa in his old Chevy pickup, wisely leaving his own county car with the Tax Assessor insignia on the door panel at the office.

He drove straight to Guadalupe's house and knocked on the door. She answered in her bathrobe, took one look at Henry, and smiled.

"How's your boss these days?" she asked.

"I think you know how he is, Ma'am," said Henry. "I doubt he's gonna last long."

"It's his own fault," Guadalupe said.

"I know that. But the thing is, Ma'am, he's right. This house belongs to the county."

Guadalupe crossed her arms across her ample bosom and glared. "You better be careful," she said. "What your boss has might be catching."

"Yes, Ma'am, I know it," said Henry. "But that don't change the fact that this is not your house. But I have an idea."

"I'm listening."

"Well, if this is the county's house, and it is, then we can do anything we want with it. We can sell it..."

"No way, pendejo."

"Or," Henry continued, "we can auction it off."

"You don't look so good," said Guadalupe. "I think maybe you already caught that disease. Maybe you should go home and get into bed."

"Now listen," Henry added hastily. "If we auction off this house, we're bound to accept the highest bid. That's the law." Henry licked his lips. "So here's the deal. I'm ready to auction this house off right now, right here. We'll waive the public notice."

Guadalupe looked at him suspiciously. "Is this some kind of trick?"

"No, Ma'am." Henry looked over his shoulder. "And it seems like you might be the only bidder. So, if you care to start the bidding..."

"How much?"

"How much do you have on you?" said Henry.

Guadalupe went into the house and came back a moment later with a tin coffee can. She looked inside and hastily counted the bills. "Forty-six dollars," she said.

Henry swallowed hard. He announced to the thin air, "I am bid forty-six dollars. Is there another bid?" The two of them looked up and down the empty street. "Forty-six dollars going once, twice, three times," said Henry loudly. "Sold! For forty-six dollars." He took some forms out his pocket and filled them out, stamped them with the seal, and handed the carbon to Guadalupe. "Congratulations, Ma'am. You are the proud owner of this, um, unique fixer-upper."

Guadalupe handed Henry a wad of bills. "Tell your boss I think his condition might improve," she said, smiling grimly. Then she added, "Your boss ain't gonna like this. You tell him, he gives you any trouble he's gonna get the goddamn plague next time."

When Henry got back to his car he looked down at the wad of bills. He counted it. It was twenty-eight dollars.

A few days later, when Meeks condition disappeared as mysteriously as it had arrived, he returned to work. Henry told him about the auction.

"Who authorized an auction?"

"Well, it was our house," Henry explained.

Meeks, still weak from his ordeal, nodded impatiently. "Okay, okay," he muttered. "How much did we get?"

"Forty-six dollars," said Henry, handing his boss the paperwork.

"*What?*" Meeks shouted, then doubled over with pain. His chest was still on the mend. "How..." he gasped, "did...we get... so little?"

"Well, as you know, real estate values in that area are pretty depressed."

"Yeah... but still. How... many... bidders?"

"Oh, a bunch a folk showed up. But as you know, economic conditions in that area are pretty depressed."

Meeks nodded vaguely and walked unsteadily toward his office. When he was sitting in his chair, he looked down at the paperwork Henry had given him. He read the name of the purchaser and went red in the face.

Henry was not sorry that he had saved his boss's life, even if he got no thanks for it. The only thing that really pissed him off was that it had cost him eighteen dollars out of his own pocket to do it.

Guadalupe's defeat of the Taxman cemented her reputation as a bruja. Though the people of Espantosa feared her more than ever, they also consulted her in droves.

"Guadalupe, help me with my no-good husband who's cheating on me. Cast a spell on him and make his ganas drop off."

Or...

"Guadalupe, make my boss get off my back. Cast a spell on him and make his dick shrivel up like a dead snake."

Or...

"Guadalupe, I got a ticket for speeding. Cast a spell on that no-good Smokey the Bear and turn his dick into a rattlesnake to bite him on his ass."

Though Guadalupe never succeeded in making anyone's ganas disappear, or in turning anyone's penis into a snake, living or dead, she was nevertheless credited with every disaster that befell people in Espantosa. When Fent Hurley's roof was lifted off his house by a twister, people said he must have pissed off Guadalupe. When Benny Cantu developed cancer everyone attributed it to the fact that he had once shot the finger at Guadalupe. No matter that this event occurred when Benny was still a teenager. "That bruja," people said, "has a long memory."

Even now, whenever Guadalupe waddled out of her house, people went out of their way to be polite to her. And they still consulted her, though the old woman was hard of hearing and they had to shout their requests.

"Guadalupe," someone would say at the top of his lungs, "my stinking whore of a wife is sleeping around!"

"Who's coming around?"

"MY WIFE IS SLEEPING AROUND AGAIN! That bitch is fucking everything in sight!"

"Ah," Guadalupe would say, nodding her head.

Chapter Five

In fact, Melchor had long considered the idea of a yearly festival. He knew of other small towns that had managed to stage events of this sort, from spinach or strawberry festivals to watermelon thumps. Why not Espantosa? The problem had always been, what to promote?

At first, he regretted having blurted out his idea for the festival. What was he thinking? And two weeks? How could he plan a festival in two weeks, especially one that didn't exist? But the more he thought about it, the more it seemed that the advent of the Book called for just this kind of decisive action. He decided to call together a meeting of some of the town's leading citizens. For lack of a better location, the meeting was held at The Beer Haus.

The Beer Haus was Espantosa's only drinking establishment. Melchor had learned from experience that there was no use calling a meeting at the Baptist church or the Rialto, both of which lent themselves better to a public forum. No one would come. The great advantage of the Beer Haus was that people who attended could order a cold beer. A few drinks made everyone more social, more open to new ideas, and, in some cases, bolder. Maybe, he reflected, that was why sheriffs of the Old West always drew their posses from the patrons of the local saloon.

The Beer Haus was built in the late 1940s, by Hermann Grossbeck who was an Army supply clerk in Vienna after the war. Grossbeck, who had been born and raised in Espantosa, reportedly opened the Beer Haus on money he'd made selling goods to Austrians on the black market. The décor was a mixture of Old Vienna and the Southwest. Framed prints of Viennese landmarks hung beside faded posters of the Alamo and Emiliano Zapata. On a shelf behind the bar ceramic beer steins rubbed shoulders with ancient longneck beer bottles. A bust of Strauss stood at one end of the bar, a statue of Cantiflas at the other. The jukebox contained almost as many Strauss waltzes as Hank Williams tunes.

When Grossbeck died he left the establishment to his son, Hermann Junior who, for reasons no one could remember, was known as Small Bill. Small Bill was actually a large man, ham-fisted and broad shouldered, with a beefy face and a crew cut. He looked like an overgrown G.I. Joe. He kept the Beer Haus running, and even managed to put aside enough money to take a yearly trip to Las Vegas or Lake Charles, where he prudently gambled as much as he could afford to lose, and sometimes even won. When Melchor asked to hold the meeting, Small Bill agreed happily, not from civic mindedness, but from the expectation of increased beer sales if everyone showed up.

In the end, it was a small gathering. Mendoza was forced to admit that when it came to leading citizens, Espantosa was in short supply. Among those present were Mrs. Nelson and her son, Bruce, Gorman Price, Connie Mays, Bill French, Pastor Gill, Fent Hurley and a few others. Two teenage boys were playing pool at the back of the room, and Sheriff Polk was sipping a beer at the bar. Melchor took a long look at the assembly, sighed heavily, and began.

"As you all know," he said, "the arrival of Miss Coakely has afforded us with a rare opportunity."

"What's that?" Gorman poked, grinning.

Mendoza scowled. "We have a chance, maybe this one chance, to put Espantosa on the map. I, for one, seriously doubt inventing stories about movie stars is gonna do the trick." There was general laughter. "We need a bona fide reason to make people want to come to Espantosa," he added emphatically. There was a nervous silence. "This is where I need your help."

"Hell, Melchor," said Hurley, "we all know no one ever comes to Espantosa 'less they're lost or passing through."

"All that's gonna change," said Mendoza confidently.

"How you figure on doing that?" asked Gorman.

"A festival," Mendoza announced. This was greeted with loud guffaws from the pool players, who had been listening in, and a horrendous belch from Sheriff Polk.

"Not that again?" said Hurley. "You been on about that for ten years. Ain't nothing in Espantosa worth celebrating."

"I think we should hear Mr. Mendoza out," said the Pastor.

"Thank you, Pastor Gill," said Mendoza. "Now what I'm proposing is a yearly festival, a celebration of some aspect of life here in our fair city..."

"Our fair what?" said Gorman.

"In our fair city," Melchor continued. "Now ya'll know there's all sorts of ridiculous festivals held throughout the state, from Tumbleweed Days to the rattlesnake hunt. I don't see why we can't put on as good a show here in Espantosa."

"What would we celebrate?" asked Mrs. Nelson.

"Well, that's where I need your help. I've given the matter a lot of thought, and I know if we put our heads together, we can come up with something." There was an uncomfortable silence. "There *must* be something!"

"I know," Gorman exclaimed. "We can have the Dirt Festival. We sure got plenty o' that around here."

"Got a lot of flies, too," Hurley guffawed.

"And mosquitoes."

"Be serious people," Mendoza pleaded. "Folks aren't gonna drive all the way from San Antonio to see flies. They got plenty of their own."

"I think we can rule out any agricultural theme," said Mr. Rigby, who taught science at the high school. "That has to be seasonal, besides which we don't have any agriculture to speak of."

Fent Hurley huffed. There was a longstanding feud between Hurley and Rigby. The science teacher argued that use of chemical fertilizers could increase crops while Hurley maintained Rigby was "a damn fool who'll poison us all."

"Might as well admit it, Melchor," said Gorman, "we got nothing to celebrate."

"What about a food theme?" said Connie . "I mean, there's all kinds of food festivals, aren't there? Maybe we could have something like that."

Deputy Polk burped loudly again and several people snickered at the timing.

"Ain't nobody gonna drive ten miles to sample Roy's chili," Gorman smirked. Roy's chili was a standing joke in Espantosa. It was greasy and grisly and usually resulted in a bad case of the runs. The only person who really liked it was Roy. He made a pot every Wednesday and ate most of it himself.

"We don't grow nothin', we don't make nothin', and we sure as hell don't have nothin'," he continued. "In fact, that's just about all we do have, plenty o' nothin'. Let's face it," said Gorman with undisguised relish, "Espantosa is the asshole of Texas."

"I'll drink to that," said Polk.

Melchor's spirits sank. He looked at Connie. She smiled back at him weakly.

"All we need," he said quietly and firmly, "is ganas."

"Balls?" said Gorman.

"He's right," said Connie, rising to her feet and moving to stand beside Mendoza. "Balls is just what we need." Gorman snickered and Sheriff Polk shifted uncomfortably atop his bar stool. Connie turned to Melchor and beamed. "Prairie oysters," she said.

"What the hell?" said Fent Hurley.

"Prairie oysters," Connie repeated. "Why not? They've got festivals for just about everything else in Texas. I tried them once, at the Folklife Festival in San Antonio. They're not bad, once you get past the idea of what you're eating."

"Well, that's about the craziest idea we come up with yet," said Polk. "And on that note, I'm goin' home."

"No," Melchor said. "She's right. Why not prairie oysters? It's so crazy it might just work."

Mrs. Nelson leaned toward her son, Bruce. "What are prairie oysters?"

Bruce leaned over and whispered in her ear.

"Oh, my!" she gasped.

On Wednesdays, Melchor's routine was to check the Soft Soap, the Laundromat he'd inherited along with Rialto from his aunt. The Soft Soap was Melchor's main source of income. Combined with the meager ticket sales and the monthly rent the Pastor paid, the quarters from the Laundromat kept him in groceries, paid the bills, and even allowed him to save enough to pay his yearly property tax. But he knew it was only a matter of time before the last machines broke down for good. Originally, there were twelve washers and eight driers, but only eight of the washers were in working order and half the driers were beyond repair. He could hear the death rattle in one of the driers each time he checked it. He wondered how much money he'd lose when the machine finally went out.

On his way to the Laundromat that morning, Melchor considered how much there was to do if the festival was going to be a success. He realized he was going to need money. A lot of money. This thought depressed him, because he knew there was only one place he could go for financial help, and it was a long shot at best.

When Melchor got to the Soft Soap he found that one of the washers was leaking water. He inspected the hoses and discovered a leak. He took a hose off one of the defunct washers and replaced the bad one. To his surprise, it worked. He then set about mopping up the mess, after which he emptied the coins from each machine, collected some stray socks and a pair of yellowed underwear from the driers, and tossed these into the wastebasket.

Melchor walked back to the Rialto, his pockets jingling with quarters.

As he approached the theater, he saw Danny Montez waiting outside. Danny, a skinny high school student with caramel colored eyes, was unusual because, of all the patrons of the Rialto, Danny was the only person who actually came to see the movie.

On the nights Danny attended, Melchor fired up the popcorn machine, which he rarely used otherwise. Danny would sit in the same seat every time, munching popcorn, entirely oblivious to the carnal happenings around him, his eyes riveted on the screen, his lips moving in unison with the lines being spoken.

Occasionally, Melchor reminded Danny that the movie he loved so much was not the *real* French Connection. Over the years, the film had worn, been cut and spliced, so that now it was missing significant portions. Danny did not mind. "I like it like this," he told Melchor. "It's still great."

"Don't you ever get tired of watching the same movie over and over?" Melchor asked him once.

"Never," Danny stated flatly. "It's the greatest movie ever made."

There were times, swayed by the fervency of Danny's opinion, Melchor considered showing the same movie over and over, night after night, year after year, might be a sort of tribute to its greatness. In his heart, however, he knew the movie he projected onto the faded screen was, if anything, a travesty.

As Melchor approached the Rialto, Danny waved to him and grinned. "Man, I can't believe this shit." he said. "You wanna serve up cow testicles and call it a festival?"

"Cows don't have testicles," Melchor reminded him.

"Oh, yeah. You know what I mean."

Danny followed Melchor into the theater. They went into the tiny office and Melchor emptied the quarters into a paper sack.

"You get your allowance this week?" he asked.

"Nah," Danny admitted. He perched himself on top of the iron desk. "Report card."

Melchor gave him a handful of quarters.

"Thanks, man."

"You keep getting these lousy grades, you're not going to graduate. Then how you gonna get out of this place?"

"Na, man. It's my teachers. They don't like me."

Melchor shrugged. He knew Danny had behavior problems, but he didn't figure it was his job to parent the boy. "As long as you graduate."

"I will, I will." He took one of the quarters and tossed it into the air, catching it neatly on the back of his hand. "Heads, this festival goes down in history as the biggest flop ever. Tails, Espantosa becomes the cow testicle capital of Texas."

"Tails," said Melchor, ignoring Danny's failure to grasp bovine anatomy.

Danny uncovered the coin and winked. "Don't feel bad, Melchor, my man. We lose either way."

Despite the unresolved issue of financing the festival, Melchor felt it necessary to push forward with his plans. He organized a clean-up crew made up of the town's ill-fated high school football team. The school itself was so small that in some years they had not been able to field a full team, and in the years they did, the result was nearly always disastrous.

If the Titan football team was an embarrassment, they did have one thing to be proud of: their football field. It was an anomaly. Unlike the rest of Espantosa, the field was meticulously maintained all year round by a man named Santiago Morales. Visiting teams often gasped upon first seeing the perfectly manicured emerald green grass, the brightly painted bleachers, and the silver goal posts shining in the sun. They soon lost their awe when the Titans took the field.

Santiago had cared for the field for so long, and done such an outstanding job, year after year, that the board of trustees actually named it after him. Santiago was honored, until he saw the sign erected over the scoreboard. It read: Santiago Morales Memorial Field.

"But I'm not dead, pendejos!" he exclaimed.

Toby Knight, who headed the school board, took him aside and explained.

"Santiago, no one ever names a field after someone until they're dead. It wouldn't look right."

The real reason for the sign being that way was that the board figured Santiago couldn't last much longer (he was well past seventy) and they did not want to have to repaint the sign after his demise.

Despite the glorious playing field, the Espantosa Titans had not won a game in over nine years, and this year looked to be no exception. The team had already played two games and had failed to score in either of them. As Melchor watched three boys attempting to remove a tattered awning from the old Sears catalog center, he could see why. The boys managed to tear the awning down in large strips, leaving tattered pieces of green tarp hanging limply from the wire frame, which they had bent so badly in the process it also had to be removed.

Several children were sitting on the broken curb watching the escapades of the football team and laughing. Melchor sat down beside them, resisting the urge to put his head in his hands and moan. One of the children, a girl named Gloria Tilden, looked up at Melchor and smiled. "Are you gonna clean up the whole town?" she asked.

"That's the plan."

"My daddy says you're a damn fool."

"Your daddy's right, I think."

"Can I have a quarter?"

Melchor reached into his pocket and fished out a quarter. He handed it to the girl who stared at it uncertainly.

"Can I have two?" she asked.

The other children, who had witnessed this exchange, began to clamor for quarters of their own. Melchor shook his head and got to his feet. "If you want a quarter each, then you go down the street picking up all the trash you see."

"You *gave* her a quarter," one of the boys accused.

"That was a free sample."

"Man, forget you!" The children left, grumbling. When they were at a safe distance, one of the boys turned and gave Melchor the finger.

Chapter Six

If most people in Espantosa were skeptical about the upcoming festival, at least one person seemed to be in Melchor's corner from the start. Not only did Connie offer to handle all the publicity for the event, she even volunteered to help clean up the old Gazette offices. Melchor intended to use the space as a central location for all things relating to the festival. But when he showed up the next morning and opened the place, his heart sank. He had not been inside the building for a long time and was shocked at how filthy it was. The floor was covered in dust and animal droppings. The walls were mildewed. There was a large nest of yellow jackets in one corner of the ceiling. The enormous press, which occupied most of the space, was covered in a dusty shroud. To make matters worse, Melchor knew that somewhere under the silent hulk was the skeleton of a cat. This simple fact greatly unnerved him.

"It looks like we have our work cut out for us," said Connie.

Melchor turned sharply. He had not heard her approach. She stood in the doorway dressed in blue jeans and a t-shirt and carrying a bucketfull of cleaning supplies, a broom and a mop. "Yeah," he admitted. "I didn't know it was this awful."

"Oh, it's not so bad. Just needs a little elbow grease."

Melchor looked doubtful. "Maybe I should just work out of the Rialto," he said.

"Nah. This will be much better." Connie located the bathroom and began filling the bucket with soapy water. "You can start with the windows," she called over her shoulder. "Windex is here."

"Paper towels?"

"Use newspaper. Works better anyway."

Melchor looked around the room and found a dusty pile of old papers in one corner. He picked them up, blew the dust off, and stared down at the headline. He laughed out loud.

"Wanna let me in on it?" asked Connie, emerging from the bathroom.

Melchor picked up the paper and showed her the headline: *Mendoza Wins by Landslide.* "I guess this one was not a big seller," he smirked. "Well, at least it can be put to use now." He crumpled the paper into a fist-sized wad and began to work on the windows.

They worked steadily for the better part of the morning. At one point, Connie paused and said under her breath, "Jesus, you gotta see this."

Melchor joined her behind Umberto's ancient desk. He peered into an open drawer. Six yellowed teeth lay at the bottom.

"Yeah," he said. "Those are Umberto's."

"What was he saving them for, the Tooth Fairy?"

By noon, even Connie was forced to admit fatigue. She pulled two sandwiches out of a paper sack and a bottle of Ozarka. "We'll have to share," she said, taking a sip and handing the bottle to Melchor. "I must look like shit."

She had pulled back her hair and her cheeks were high in color. Her t-shirt was damp and clung to her, accentuating the fullness of her breasts. "You look great," said Melchor with a seriousness that made Connie laugh.

Connie took a bite of her sandwich and said, chewing, "This place isn't that bad, you know. You never thought of running the paper again?"

"No," said Melchor. "I'm not even sure the press would run after all these years. It was temperamental to start with. You should have seen Umberto when he had an issue to put out. He cursed up a storm and one time even broke a toe kicking it."

"How is he?"

Melchor took a sip of water and shook his head. "I have no idea. Haven't seen him in years."

"You should."

"You're right." Melchor stood up and began to pace the room. "I was thinking..."

"That'll get you in trouble."

"Maybe if we let Roy do the cooking, we could convince Helen to put up some cash."

Connie winced. "You want Roy to do the cooking? You'll poison half the county."

Melchor waved his hand. "I know, I know. But I can't imagine how we're going to pay for everything."

"You really think Helen will come through. You're not exactly the flavor of the month with that woman."

"I don't suppose you'd come with me?"

"I'm no more her darling than you are," Connie protested. Melchor gave her a sheepish grin and she smiled. "Okay, okay. I'll go."

Guadalupe had learned about the arrival of Miss Coakely that very morning when Tonio

60

Cruz came by in his pickup to haul off the aluminum cans she'd collected that week. Tonio was a young man who was distantly related to Guadalupe. The relation was not clear, but Tonio always referred to the old woman as Tia nonetheless.

"There's a stranger in town," he said, picking up the green plastic garbage bags from Guadalupe's front porch. "Some girl writing a book."

"A book?" Guadalupe's curiosity was rarely aroused. Most of what people thought was interesting or salacious she found simply boring. It was not the arrival of the girl, therefore, that interested her but the mention of the Book. "What kind of book?"

"A guide book," Tonio replied. Then, in response to Guadalupe's impatient glare: "It's a book that tells people about places they never been." He tossed the bags into the back of his pickup. "So I guess everyone's gonna wanna read this one cause ain't no one ever been here!"

Guadalupe turned back into her house. Though she knew people read books, she had never yet heard of anyone writing one. Guadalupe could neither read nor write, and she regarded books as mystical objects, the secrets of which were permanently hidden from her. She sat down on a ragged armchair and picked up a handful of sunflower seeds. She expertly shelled the seeds in her mouth and spit the shells onto the floor. When she done this for some time, she leaned over and stared at the pattern of shells on the floor and shook her head. "Ay, Dios mio," she sighed. "What kind of trouble is coming now?"

Flora Esperanza was the prettiest girl in Espantosa. She was sixteen years old and still a virgin. For the past year, she had resisted the efforts of Tom Cade to change that status. Tom had invited her many times to go to the Rialto. Among the students of Sam Houston High, "going to the Rialto" was synonymous with losing one's cherry. Flora knew many girls who had been, and several who had gone with Tom, and she had no desire to join their ranks. She liked Tom, who was one of the most popular boys in school, and she liked to kiss him, but she was not about to risk getting pregnant like Lily Cantu. Lily was the same age as Flora and had a three month old daughter.

This afternoon, Flora was lying on her stomach on her bed, sipping Big Red soda through a straw and painting her fingernails. Her Walkman was on the bed in front of her, and she was listening to a Cristina Aguilera CD she'd bought last weekend at the mall in Carrizo Springs. As she listened, she swayed her legs, being careful not to let them touch the bedspread because her toenails were not yet dry.

Looking out the open window, she saw Danny Montez walking across the street toward her house. Danny lived next door to her, in a small house Flora's mother called "an eyesore." Though she had known Danny all her life, Flora never considered him a friend, at least not since they were little. She knew Danny had a crush on her, but this was nothing unusual; most boys had a crush on her. For her part, she thought Danny was nice looking, but too weird to ever entertain the thought of dating. First there was the fact that he was nuts about old, really old movies, even those in black and white. Then there was his friendship with Melchor Mendoza, which kind of made sense because of the movie connection, maybe. Finally, there was the matter of his hat. Danny had worn a porkpie hat ever since middle school, the same, he reminded anyone who asked, as Gene Hackman wore in *The French Connection*. No, Danny was definitely not dating material, not unless Flora ever decided to commit social suicide.

Now, as Danny approached her side of the street, he glanced up and saw her through the window. He waved and Flora waved listlessly back at him. Christ, she thought, don't let him come over. But Danny, as if summoned by her wave, threw one leg over the fence, straddled it momentarily, then pulled the other leg after him. He walked over to the window.

"Heard the news?" he asked, leaning on the window sill.

Flora took off her headphones. "What did you say?"

"Did you hear the news?" Danny repeated. "About the festival."

"Oh. Yeah." Flora blew on her fingernails. "Pretty lame, huh?"

"I think it's great," said Danny. Flora rolled her eyes. "I mean, it's so perfect. I wish I had a camera."

"A camera?"

"It would make a great documentary."

Flora had seen documentaries before in school. She couldn't imagine the word "great" being used to describe any of those.

"You know it's going to be a total disaster."

"Why should it be a disaster?"

"Come on," Danny grinned. "This is Espantosa."

Flora wrinkled her nose. It was a recent habit, and one that her mother did not approve of at all. "I guess," she said, flipping through her CDs, being careful not to smudge her polish. She was ready for him to leave now. She certainly didn't want anyone to pass by at this moment and see Danny Montez leaning on *her* window sill.

Danny showed no signs of leaving, so Flora put another CD into her walkman and slipped on the earphones. She looked up at him and smiled, as if to say, Thank you very much for coming by, you may now go. After a moment, he took the hint, tipped his hat and left.

Looking down at her hand, Flora noticed with chagrin that she had smudged a nail.

Danny slipped quietly into the back door of his house. His mother, he knew, would be asleep at this time of the day. She worked nights at the Pak-N- Sip, a 24 hour convenience store located on the interstate. Danny's father had walked out the front door six months ago to buy a pack of cigarettes. He had never returned. Danny knew he had taken up with a woman in Crystal City, and he still ran into him from time to time. He had never really blamed his father for leaving. His mother was a terror to live with. As he saw it, they were never happy together, and at least now that his father was gone, the fights had stopped. His only regret was that he no longer had an ally in the house. His sister, Melissa, was seven, and her mother doted on her. Now that it was just the three of them, Danny had to bear the full brunt of her vicious tongue. It was one reason he spent so many nights at the Rialto.

He opened the refrigerator and took out a piece of bologna and a tortilla. He turned on the stove and laid the tortilla on the burner. Then he put the bologna in a pan with some oil and began to fry it.

His sister, drawn by the aroma of the bologna, padded into the kitchen dragging a stuffed gorilla behind her. She looked at him accusingly.

"Mom said we're not supposed to eat anything before dinner," she said. "I'm telling."

"Shut up," said Danny.

"You said shut up. I'm telling about that, too."

"You want me to make you a taco, don't you?"

Melissa hesitated. She peered into the pan. "That's only one piece," she said.

"I can make another piece, but you have to be quiet and not tell Mom."

"It's a deal," said Melissa. Danny knew as soon as she had her taco she would forget the deal, but he didn't really care. His mother was bound to notice the missing piece of bologna anyway. She always kept strict account of all the foodstuffs in the house. Since she started her diet, she decided Danny and Melissa needed to watch what they ate, too. When Danny protested that she was the one with the weight problem, not him, she had lectured him vehemently on the importance of establishing good eating habits early in life. Her diligence was always lax when it came to Melissa, who was already a chunky little thing and well on her way to being as obese as her mother.

When the tacos were done, Danny gave one to Melissa on a napkin and took his into the living room. He picked up the remote and changed the station.

"Hey," cried Melissa. "I was watching that!"

"I made the tacos," Danny reminded her. "So I get to pick the station."

Melissa sat down on the couch and bit into her taco, glaring at him.

Danny flipped through a few channels. Espantosa had only recently got cable, and the company was not a good one. His mother refused to purchase more than the basic package, so the choice of viewing was limited. After some searching, Danny found a documentary on the mob and settled into his father's armchair, the only item in the house that had belonged to him and *not* been tossed onto the lawn the day after he left.

Danny ate his taco, enjoying the taste of the bologna which he had browned almost to the point of burning. He watched the show, but his mind was still on Flora, and the sight of her bare legs, the flaming pink toenails. Danny had a tendency to cast the people in his life as he would a film, and in his mind Flora was definitely the love interest. The problem was, try as he might, he could never find it in him to cast himself as the romantic lead playing opposite her. He knew no audience would believe it.

As predicted, as soon as Melissa finished her taco she began to whine and threaten to tell on Danny if he didn't change the channel back. He tossed her the remote and left the room. There was no sense in letting her wake up his mother.

In his room, Danny took off his shirt and stretched out on his bed. It was hot, but he knew better than to turn on the air conditioner. The only room that was air-conditioned these days was the room where his mother and Melissa slept.

The notion of shooting a documentary had not really occurred to him until he told Flora. Now it seemed like a great idea. He wondered if he could find a camera. He knew he wouldn't be able to shoot with film, but perhaps he could use videotape. The school, he knew, had two video cameras and an editing machine. It was part of the equipment they had purchased with Title I money. The school received these funds because more than half the students qualified for free lunch. Actually, nearly every student did. It was for this reason that Sam Houston High housed two computer labs and a technology center, though the school's aging electrical infrastructure often failed, rendering the labs useless. This year, Danny's science class had visited the lab only to have a power outage shut it down. Rather than produce Powerpoint presentations, Mr. Rigby had the students complete their projects with posterboard and crayons.

The Technology Center was off limits to students, but Danny had helped a teacher pick up equipment once. It was little more than an oversized closet filled with everything from overhead projectors to laptop computers. He also noted three camcorders in hard plastic cases and two tripods. There was even some lighting equipment. More importantly, there was an editing machine.

Teachers rarely used the Technology Center either. Few of them were technologically proficient. In fact, probably the only person at Sam Houston High who was dying to get his hands on the equipment was Danny. The problem was: how could he do it?

Danny began to sweat. The room was especially hot because the air conditioner, which he was forbidden to use, was lodged in the only window in the room. He reached over and turned on the oscillating fan with his toe.

His only chance at getting a camera, he knew, was to convince a teacher to check it out for him. That seemed unlikely. His reputation on campus was not good. The only teacher who even seemed to tolerate him was Mr. Rigby, and even then he had written three office referrals on Danny that year.

He heard his mother moving around in the room next to his. He looked at the clock. It was nearly two, about the time she usually woke up.

Danny was certain a documentary about the first ever Prairie Oyster Festival would be a success. Two years ago, his history teacher had shown the class a movie called *Roger and Me*. Danny had thought it one of the finest and funniest films he had ever seen, though his teacher had gotten in trouble for showing it. He felt sure that, with the right angle, he could make a film along the same lines. Though he knew that a good video was never as highly regarded as a good movie shot with a real camera and real film, he thought if it was successful it might help him get into film school at UT.

Melissa had apparently heard her mother, because she thumped down the hall and knocked on her door. A moment later, Danny heard the sound of their muffled voices. He heard his mother's voice rise sharply. Melissa was telling.

Chapter Seven

Amanda Coakely had spent the better part of the day asleep. When she finally arose, used the restroom, and walked into the kitchen, she found a plate covered with a napkin sitting on the table. There was a note beside the plate that read: *Mr. Gill and I will be out this morning. Please enjoy your breakfast. If you have to go out, you may leave the house unlocked.* She removed the napkin from the plate and sat down to eat. In the end, she only picked at the food. The note had unnerved her. It made her feel too much like someone's child. The final phrase, in particular—*you may leave the house unlocked*—troubled her vaguely. Miss Coakely was not accustomed to being trusted so easily.

Yet trust was an integral part of her "business." From town to town, for nearly six years, Miss Coakely had perfected the art of manufacturing trust. It was a skill she'd acquired early in life. When she was twelve, her mother moved out and left her with a man she thought was her father. She discovered the truth when he attempted to register her for the new school year. He was unable to sign the necessary forms. He could not prove legal custody. Rather than become a ward of the state, Amanda fled, first to an aunt's house, then to the home of a distant cousin. By the age of fourteen, she discovered she preferred life on the street to the dismal existence her relatives provided her. She could not stand being anybody's poor relation. She slipped out of the house late one night, after pocketing the sixty-four dollars cash in her cousin's purse.

What followed were several years of living hand to mouth, bouncing from shelters to flop houses to bus stations and underpasses. And there were men, of course there were men. Old men who pawed at her like some exotic pet, young men who fucked her like jackrabbits and abandoned her as soon as they grew tired of her. She had more than a few scrapes with the law, but always the officers would look at her skinny legs and bony elbows, her dark, moist eyes, too large for such a small face, and they would let her off with a warning, sometimes even handing her a few bills, a handful of change.

Then she met Rudolph. Rudolph was a photographer, tall and muscular, with stone-gray hair and a great black mustache. He found Amanda lurking in a doorway in downtown San Antonio. As he approached her, she stepped out into the light and gazed at him boldly. He smiled and waved her forward.

"How old are you?" he asked.

"Nineteen," she lied.

"I see, I see," he said, looking up and down the decrepit street. "Not such a nice place for a young girl to be late at night."

"I can take care of myself."

"I'm sure you can." He reached into his pocket and took out a twenty-dollar bill. "Do you want to earn some money?"

"Depends," she sniffed.

"It's not what you think," he smiled. He had beautiful white teeth. "I want to take pictures of you."

"Naked?" she asked. "That'll cost you more."

"You can keep your clothes on," he laughed. "I just want you to take off your shoes."

"My shoes?"

"I just want to photograph your feet. That's what I do."

"Some kind of pervert?"

"If you like. I'll pay you twenty dollars just to take off your shoes."

Amanda hesitated. Suddenly, she felt shy, more so than if he had asked her to take off her clothes then and there. "I don't know," she said.

"It will only take a few minutes."

"My feet are dirty."

"I don't mind." He really had the whitest teeth she had ever seen.

She bit her lip, looked down at her shoes, and then reached down and slipped them off.

"Very nice. Very good. You have pretty feet, you know?" Rudolph took out his camera. "Very pretty."

Amanda reached out and snatched the bill from his hand.

Over the next several weeks, Rudolph came to see her often, and eventually he invited her to his house. It was located in the Hill Country at the top of a canyon, surrounded by Mountain Cedar. The house was enormous and richly furnished. The walls were hung with dozens of photographs taken all over the world.

"Did you take all these pictures?" she asked, standing shyly in the middle of the living room.

"Not all of them. Most of them."

Amanda examined the room more closely. "You got all this from taking pictures?"

"Yes."

"I thought you only took pictures of girls' feet."

"That," said Rudolph, "is my hobby."

"Pretty strange hobby."

"I suppose so."

Amanda took off her shoes and settled down on the sofa beside him. "So, did you bring me here to take more pictures, or what?"

"Why don't you come with me?"

He led her down the hallway to an enormous room with walls so white it hurt her eyes to look at them. He opened a closet and smiled. "Why don't you pick out a pair? I think you'll find some in your size."

The closet was filled with dozens of pairs of women's shoes. Amanda laughed. "This is some big thing with you, isn't it?"

"You could say that."

For the next several hours, Amanda tried on pair after pair of shoes. Rudolph took dozens of photos. When she finally admitted fatigue, he made her breakfast and they sat together on the enormous patio and watched the sun rise.

"Are you going to take me back now?" she asked.

"Not unless you're in a hurry. You can stay."

"I'd like that," she said.

"But there's only the one bed."

"I don't mind."

Despite her expectations, Rudolph did not make love to her that night, or any other night. They slept in the same bed, but not only did he make no sexual advances, he resisted the few times she attempted to initiate things. Then one night Amanda woke to pee and found the bed empty beside her. As she approached the

73

bathroom, she heard the sound of soft moans through the half-open door. She did not approach. A few minutes later, Rudolph returned to bed and nestled close beside her.

Amanda stayed with Rudolph for nearly seven months. She was surprised at how solitary his life was. He seemed to have no friends, and the phone rarely rang. Sometimes he would go out at night, but never did he bring another woman home. She was often bored, and took to reading the books in Rudolph's enormous library. Whenever he found her reading, he would laugh and cajole her. "You're becoming a true bookworm," he warned. Then he would discourse for long periods on the virtues of this author over that author, often reading passages aloud.

Finally, near the end of October, Rudolph announced that he had accepted an assignment in Chiapas.

"Do you have to go?"

"It's time to earn some money again," he said wearily. "It can't be helped. Every paradise has its price."

"I understand," she said quietly.

"You don't have to go," he said, laying his hand on her knee. "I'll only be gone a few weeks. I can leave you some money, and there's the car. Can you drive?"

Amanda nodded. "I can take care of myself," she said.

"That's funny," he said. "That was one of the first things you said to me."

The next day, he left. Amanda intended to wait for him, but she found the empty house spooked her. After the third day, she took the money he'd left her and the keys to his car. She drove the car into San Antonio and sold it on the West Side to a dealer who asked no questions. She bought the cheapest car on the lot and drove away with close to two thousand dollars in her pocket.

She had been on the road ever since. She kept to the smaller towns, and sometimes she stayed long enough to find work, usually as a waitress or clerking in a store. Then she read an ad in a magazine looking for "bold adventurers" to "write exotic travelogues." This was the beginning of her new career, the one that had led her through small towns across the Southwest and, eventually, to Espantosa.

And now she was stuck. It was not the first time, nor it would it be the last. But she knew from experience that if she was going to move on, she had better do so soon. That meant earning someone's trust, but just whose she was not yet sure.

Of course, there was the Mayor. He was a complete buffoon, a real Bambolini, but that was just the trouble. People like that were hard to figure. In Miss Coakely's experience, most people had hidden motives, and all she had to do was discover what that motive was and she was halfway home. Mendoza, on the other hand, might be just what he seemed. Did he really believe this shithole town could be any better than it was? Could he be that naïve?

Yes, she decided firmly, he could. It was a place to start.

She bit off the end of a slice of toast and went to her room to dress. She had a lot to do and very little time.

Connie's father Howard was the town's banker. They had once lived in the nicest home in town, the very house, in fact, now occupied by Helen and Roy Blas. When the ruin began to hit the town, it seemed for a time the Mays family would be spared. Connie could clearly remember that winter day when she rode her bike from school and turned up the driveway to her house. Suddenly, she felt the shadow of enormous wings above her, and turning sharply saw a giant owl disappear over the treetops. She rushed inside to tell her mother about what she'd seen. As soon as she entered the house, she felt something was wrong. Her father was home. He was sitting at the kitchen table with her mother, and from the look on their faces, Connie was sure someone had died. Her mother looked up at her and motioned her away. The last thing Connie saw was her mother's arm resting on the slumped shoulders of her father. It would be several days before she learned fully what had happened.

After the collapse of the bank, Howard Mays was never the same. The family went through their savings quickly, sold their home and moved into a trailer. Connie listened to her father make endless plans, none of which bore fruit. In the evenings, he often stood in the back yard and gazed up at the stars as though the secret to his destiny lay hidden there. The night before he died, Connie approached him during his reverie, and heard her father whispering, "The lone and level sands stretch far away."

Connie's father had been dead now for nearly a decade, but over the years she'd spent in cities as far away as Denver and Tucson, whenever she was going through a tough time, she found herself standing under the stars remembering those words, sometimes repeating them softly to herself. She never knew what it was her father meant, or what those words meant to him, but the invocation never failed to calm her. And when she was tempted to think of the life she'd given up to come home and care for her mother, the image of those lone and level sands brought her strange comfort.

As they approached the Blas house, Melchor noticed Connie twice paused to look over her shoulder.

"See something?" he asked.

"No." But Connie was clearly uneasy. Melchor had not considered coming back to the house she grew up in might be painful for her.

"I should have come by myself," Melchor said. He reached down and gave her hand a squeeze. To his surprise, she did not let go. They walked together hand in hand to the front door and Melchor rang the bell.

Helen Blas had been in bed all day when she heard the doorbell. She had had a bad night, a worse day, and the last thing she needed were visitors. She dragged herself out of bed and shuffled painfully to the door. As she passed the mirror in the hallway she realized without concern that she had not even combed her hair that day. She knew she had let her looks go since the accident, but then Roy had put on considerable weight since opening the café. When it came to dressing up, or sometimes even dressing, Helen rarely put forward the same effort she had in her days before the bus swiped her off the sidewalk.

Despite the tepid relationship between her and Roy, Helen remained intensely possessive. She continued to believe that Roy, overweight and prematurely bald, was as attractive to the opposite sex as he had been in his youth. She was convinced that Roy had slept around in the early years of their marriage. Bedridden as she often was, she had no way to check up on Roy, and she was sure he would take advantage of the situation. The most likely target of his infidelity, she thought, was Connie. It was for this reason she was less than glad to see Connie and "that Mexican," as she always referred to Mendoza, standing on her doorstep.

"You have any idea how hard it was for me to come answer this door?" she said.

"I'm very sorry, Mrs. Blas," said Mendoza.

"Well, what you two want then?" Along with her looks, Helen had given up all pretense of civility.

"Can we come in, please?"

"I'm not dressed. Oh, hell, come on in then."

Connie felt a peculiar sense of both familiarity and strangeness upon entering her old home. It was darker than she remembered it, and more close. Helen kept the shades drawn and the furniture looked heavy and solemn in the dim light. Connie sensed the presence of old ghosts, but kept them at bay.

She had always thought it odd that Helen and Roy had purchased her old house because Helen was unable to climb stairs. It was the only two-story house in Espantosa. Some speculated that Roy had this in mind when he purchased the house. It was a well-known fact that Roy's bedroom was upstairs.

Helen led her visitors into the living room. The furniture looked as if it had just been delivered from a showroom. Every piece, down to the area rug and the coasters, matched perfectly, with one exception: a large black leather recliner. It was to this chair that Helen went, motioning her guests to sit on the sofa. She eased herself into the chair, then adjusted it slightly.

"Well, what is it you want?"

Melchor looked at Connie. "It's like this, Mrs. Blas. I'm sure you've heard about the festival. We need some capital, an initial investment, to purchase the, uh..." Melchor realized suddenly how ridiculous it sounded.

"We need to buy some balls," Connie interjected.

"I see," Helen said with a smirk. "I always thought the people in this town needed more of those."

"We also need to cover other expenses," Melchor said, "such as advertising, some light construction, such as the booths for food sales, a stage."

"I see. And how much money do you want for all this?"

Melchor took a deep breath. He quickly calculated, then doubled the figure. "I think four thousand dollars should cover it all."

Helen's eyes widened. "That a lot of money, Mr. Mayor."

"Yes, but I'm sure you'll earn it back. Why with food sales alone, we should..."

"Who's selling the food? I mean, who's doing the cooking?"

"Well, that hasn't been decided yet," Connie said.

"Why not Roy?"

"We just thought," said Connie, "that he had enough on his hands what with running the café and..."

"And taking care of a crippled wife?"

"That's not what I was going to say," Connie bristled.

"All right," said Helen, adjusting the chair once more and wincing. "I'll give you the money. Roy does the cooking, understood?"

Melchor looked at Connie. "Understood," he said.

"Get my checkbook. It's in the top drawer of the desk in the hallway."

Connie went to fetch the checkbook and Mrs. Blas looked at Melchor. "I think this festival scheme of yours is a damn fool idea," she scowled. "But I always said I'd pay good money to see you fall flat on your face."

Melchor met her gaze. "And what if the festival is a success?"

"Well then I guess the joke's on me," she said, handing the check to Melchor.

"My father planted these cypresses," said Connie as they left the house. "I used to look at them from my window. I always wanted to climb up to the very top. I guess you could see for miles from up there."

"A bird's eye view."

"Maybe that's why my father planted them. He had a poet's soul. People would never have believed it but he was always reading poetry. I think he even wrote some."

"I never knew."

"After the bank failed, he used to come out here and look at the stars. He said something I've always remembered."

"What did he say?"

"I feel silly talking this way," said Connie. She gave a loose shrug with one shoulder. "He said: 'The lone and level sands stretch far away.' I always wondered what it meant."

Melchor looked up at the top of the cypresses. "You know," he said softly, "sometimes, you don't have to climb all the way to the top to imagine what it looks like."

Connie looked at him frankly. "Wouldn't it be nice if that was true."

Chapter Eight

On the long Sunday afternoons of his childhood, Melchor's favorite place to be was the Rialto. He loved the cool dark of the theater, and the strange sense of solitude that he felt even when the showing was crowded.

Melchor sank into the darkness and felt the world fall away around him. Years later when his social studies teacher, Mr. Rice, told the class movies were a form of escapism, he knew exactly what he meant. He felt Mr. Rice was only partly right. Movies were only escapism for people who were looking to escape. He wondered why people in Hollywood or New York or Paris would ever go to the movies. He felt sure that if he ever made it to one of those places, he would probably never watch a movie again.

On rare occasions, Melchor would go to the movies with his father. The only films his father was interested in seeing were John Wayne westerns or anything with Lana Turner. Melchor never liked westerns. He found the desolate landscapes and the stark characters too close to home. He didn't much care for Lana Turner either.

It was on these visits to the Rialto that Melchor first found his way to the projection booth. His mother never allowed him such freedom, but his father seemed not to even notice his son once the movie began. As soon as the credits rolled, Melchor would slink out of his seat and bolt for freedom.

For ten-year-old Melchor, walking up the dark, narrow stairs to the projection booth was like ascending the stairs of heaven. The enormous projector was like the eye of God casting immortal images onto the screen. Like an acolyte of the inner temple, Melchor learned to work the magic of the projector, and was even initiated into the art of changing reels. He would usually sit in the booth with his aunt, munching chocolate and popcorn, keeping an eye on the temperamental projector, which had a tendency to seize up. If not seen-to immediately, the lens would burn through the film, and it was Melchor's job to prevent this from happening.

Melchor knew his aunt lived alone, and that people said she was rich. It would never have occurred to him that she was lonely. He was still too young to fathom the workings of the human heart. To him, Maria seemed like a character right off the screen, like a Mexican Lauren Bacall or Bette Davis, only older and less unhappy.

It was not until many years later Melchor learned that his aunt was said to have been the prettiest girl in Espantosa, and that she had once been married to Tom Walsh, the youngest son of Wallace Walsh, the oilman. Tom had moved to Espantosa in order to put some geography between himself and his father. As the story was told, he met Maria on a spring night as she walked down Houston Street in a white dress looking like a small-town version of Natalie Wood in West Side Story. The two were married a week later. Wallace, when he heard his son had married a "Mexican", was reputed to have shot his prize bull in anger.

Tom and Maria honeymooned in Acapulco. Blissful and carefree, they cavorted on the sands during the day and made love in the cabana at night. But when Tom attempted to draw from his account in the states, he was told it had been closed.

The two returned to Espantosa on a Greyhound. As his bride wept in their bedroom, Tom spent a week in furious attempts to gain control of money he had thought was his own, only to discover his father had absconded with all the funds in an apparently legal manner. By the end of the week, Maria had gone back to work at the Ben Franklin's. Over the next several months, Tom stayed home, brooded over his change in fortune, and took to drink. Increasingly belligerent to his wife, he might have beaten her to death some dark night if he had not staggered in front of an oil tanker on the interstate.

Tom Walsh's death was the cause of much discussion. No one could explain why he had walked almost seven miles from his home in a pair of ragged house slippers in the middle of the night. Then there was the fact that the tanker was carrying his father's oil. To most people this seemed like much more than a coincidence.

An inquest was held. Newspapers from as far away as Tucson had picked up on the story of young Walsh's apparent suicide. Feature stories ran for several days, and they all painted the same picture of Wallace Walsh as a cold-hearted SOB who was so mean and nasty he had caused the death of his son (indirectly) and a prize bull (directly). Wallace sent a trio of lawyers to the inquest in an attempt to squelch rumors of suicide. Curiously, Walsh also produced the allegedly dead bull, feeling perhaps that in Texas a man might be forgiven for causing the death of his own son, but he could never live down the killing of a superb animal. Whether the animal paraded before the press was the same bull he was supposed to have killed, no one questioned.

In the end, Wallace was forced to enlist the aid of Maria. On the day she was to appear at the inquest, Maria looked out the front window of her duplex and spotted a white limousine parked at the curb. She watched as a tall, heavy-set man with flowing gray hair, dressed in a black suit and carrying a white Stetson in his hand approached her front door.

"Hello, Mr. Wallace," she said, opening the door. "I been expecting you."

Whether she was or was not, her face betrayed no surprise, and surprise was something Wallace was counting on. He stooped into the doorway, paused and asked, "May I come in, Ma'am?" Though he was nearly six foot two, Wallace had no need to stoop. It was a little trick he used. When people see a tall man stooping to enter a door they automatically assume he's taller than he is. It was part of an arsenal of tricks Wallace had employed throughout his business life, just like his politeness, which always increased the more he intended to fuck you over.

Wallace entered, looked around the room and found a chair with its back against the window and sat in it. Maria sat across from him. Silhouetted against the window, Wallace's face was a shadow. She squinted at him. Wallace spread his hands across his knees and asked if he might have a drink.

"You want ice tea? I don't have anything else."

"That would be most kind of you, Ma'am," Wallace said. Another part of the arsenal. Always begin by asking your opponent for something he doesn't mind giving you, however inconsequential, because it will predispose him to keep on giving.

Maria returned with the tea. It was not, as promised, iced. It was tepid. Wallace took one sip and scowled. He ran his finger through his collar. The small oscillating fan on the floor was pointed directly at Maria. "I suppose you're wondering why I came here," he said.

"No," Maria responded flatly.

"Pardon me?"

"I know why you're here," said Maria, reaching over to switch on the lamp. "I like to see who I'm talking to," she explained.

"That's very astute, young lady," said Wallace. "But as for the purpose of my visit..."

"You want me to tell everyone that Tom was a happy man, that he loved his Papa, and that I cannot imagine any reason why he would want to quit a life so full of promise and love."

The problem with Wallace's arsenal is that it had been assembled by adopting the tactics of other men like himself over a period of many years. While such tactics worked well with less-experienced men, they had absolutely no effect on Maria. She leaned forward and said evenly and clearly, "Well, I'll tell you about your son, Mr. Walsh. He was a selfish, spoiled brat. He was a drunk and when he drank he liked to beat on me. He was sick of life and all he wanted was to join your prize bull in heaven. And that's what I'm going to tell the inquest today. Unless."

Wallace wiped the sweat from his brow. How had it gotten so hot so fast, he thought? "Unless what?" he asked.

Maria smiled. "Can I get you some ice for that tea?"

Maria opened the Rialto six months later. If Espantosa could ever be said to have had a heyday, this was it. The Aussie goat farm was thriving, and the interstate had not yet turned the motels and filling stations into ghosts, along with the people who patronized them. For a time, even the Beer Haus had competition. A pool hall, a bar, and the VFW were all in operation. The town even supported a Western Auto and a Sears Catalogue center.

The opening of the Rialto seemed to herald a period of prosperity and growth. People lined up for the first showing, and some came from as far away as Dilly and Cotulla to attend the opening. Though no one knew how much money Maria had milked from Wallace Walsh, to judge by the Rialto it had been a tidy sum. Some said one would have had to drive all the way to San Antonio or Austin to have found a more luxurious theater.

The success of the Rialto was short lived however. Shortly after it opened, the blight struck the goat farm and the Aussie vanished without a trace. A year after that, construction began on the interstate. Once it opened, the town, in the words of one resident, "shriveled up like a teat on a dead cow."

Maria would keep the theater running for another twenty years. She never remarried, and died childless, so she left the theater and the

Laundromat to Melchor. People speculated that she'd left behind a good deal more, but this was not the case. When the details of the will came out, the citizens of Espantosa were shocked to discover she'd left Melchor no more than eight hundred dollars in cash.

No one was surprised that Melchor closed the Rialto after his aunt's death. They were surprised that it had remained open as long as it had.

It was several years before Melchor discovered the enormous reels lying under the cot in the projection booth. He dusted them off and carried them over to the projector. He had threaded film so many times when his aunt was alive, but now his hands shook as he attempted the operation. He had never thought to see the screen lit up again. Before he turned on the projector, he stopped and smiled. He went downstairs and turned on the marquee. He flicked a switch and for the first time in nearly a decade, the enormous letters of The Rialto came to life.

Across the street, Roy looked out the window of the Tumbleweed Café and said, "You gotta come see this. It looks like Melchor is opening up the Rialto."

"The hell you say?"

The patrons of the café walked over to the theater. The ticket booth was dark, but inside they heard muffled sounds coming from the theater. Roy pushed open the double doors and gasped. There, in brilliant color, was Fernando Rey, striding down a crowded New York street.

"Well, I'll be damned," said Gorman Price, who was still holding his burger in his hand.

From the projection booth, Melchor peered down to see what the commotion was about. Roy, shading his eyes, called up to him, "You back in business, Melchor?"

Melchor didn't see how he could be back in business with one ragged print of *The French Connection*, but he gave him the thumbs up anyway.

Over the next few days, nearly everyone came to see the show. At first, Melchor didn't charge, but by the end of the week, he decided to open the ticket booth. To his surprise, people actually paid to get in. He even managed to fire up the old popcorn machine.

After the novelty wore off, people began to ask him what the next show would be. Melchor explained that there wouldn't be another show; he no longer had a distributor. When the novelty began to wear off, folks began to grumble. Soon it became apparent that, like everything else in Espantosa, the Rialto had had its day.

Chapter Nine

Santiago woke early, as he always did. He washed his face and dressed, then fried some eggs and chiles in a pan, made two tacos and wrapped them in foil. He had lived alone all his adult life, in the same rundown shack behind the bus garage. More than once, the school board had attempted to remove this eyesore, even offering on one occasion to build him a small house, but Santiago remained.

"If I have to move," he told them, "then I'm gonna go." He clapped his hands together and extended his right arm swiftly. "And I'm gonna keep on going," he added. The board took this to heart.

This morning, he took his tacos and walked out to the football field. It was his favorite place to eat breakfast. After all, as many people noted, it was the garden spot of Espantosa. He climbed onto the bleachers and looked out over the field. The dew on the grass caught the light of the rising sun and the whole field looked laden with silver. He smiled. He opened the foil and bit into the taco. The eggs were runny and the yolk ran down his fingers, the way he liked it. Lately, he had become fascinated with his own hands. They were large, the color of burnt cinnamon, and the fingers were as fat and wrinkled as sausages. He was proud that despite his advanced age, he had never experienced the Arthur-itis.

He was just finishing his second taco when he saw Melchor Mendoza walking across the field toward him. He had never liked Mendoza. He remembered the boy when he was in school, always stirring up trouble. He disliked him, too, because he had once attempted to do away with the football program. Mendoza had argued that in a town where water was always in short supply, it made no sense to pour it into the ground just to keep green a playing field that wasn't even used in some years.

As Mendoza approached, he waved an expansive arm that took in the whole field. "Looks great," he said.

Santiago said nothing. He blinked up at the rising sun, calculating how many hours he had before it got too hot to work.

Melchor sat down beside Santiago. He spread his hands on his knees and looked out over the field. "That's a pretty sight," he said. "No doubt about it."

"Something you want?" said Santiago.

Melchor leaned back and rested his elbows on the bleachers behind him. "I need your help," he said. He had debated on how best to approach Santiago. In the end he decided, given their history, that only simple humility would work. "I need your help, and so does the town," he added for emphasis, hoping he hadn't overdone it.

"Shit," said Santiago. "This town needs more help than I can give it." He almost added, "And the same goes for you, pendejo."

"Have you heard about the festival?"

Santiago had. The only thing that surprised him was that a Mexicano had thought of it. It seemed like the sort of thing some redneck would have come up with. Then again, he wasn't sure Mendoza was a real Mexicano. He was more of a coconut, brown on the outside, but white on the inside. He had said as much in the bus garage the morning before. When he heard that Melchor was having trouble locating enough testicles, he made a joke that was slowly working its way around Espantosa: "Everybody wants what they ain't got."

"I want to have live music," Melchor began. "It's important. But the only problem is, we need a stage."

"A stage?"

"Yes, a platform, something like that. A place where the band can set up."

Santiago had seen bands perform often at the VFW. In his experience all the band needed was a sandy floor away from the broken glass. "What you want me to do?" he asked, anxious to get this over with.

"Well, I need you to build it."

"I'm not a carpenter," Santiago protested.

"I know, but this is nothing complicated."

Santiago looked at him as if to say, if it's so damn easy why don't you do it yourself. "I'm not a carpenter," he repeated.

"But you built these bleachers, and the refreshment booth, and God knows what else."

"That was easy."

"This will be easy, too. I'll help you draw up the plans. It just has to be a platform, big enough to hold six or seven people, with an electrical outlet or two."

"I'm not an electrician."

Melchor was growing frustrated with these flat denials. "You don't have to be."

"Are you a carpenter?" Santiago asked with a gleam in his eye.

"No," Melchor said wearily. This was proving far more difficult that he thought it would be.

"Are you an electrician?"

"No."

"Then you're as good as me. So go build it yourself." Santiago climbed off the bleachers, feeling he had trapped Mendoza in a web of logic from which there was no escape.

"I can pay you!"

Santiago turned around. "How much?"

"Eight dollars an hour?"

"Ten."

"Nine."

"Fuck you, cabron."

"Okay, okay. Ten dollars an hour." Mendoza climbed off the bleachers and extended his hand. "Mrs. Nelson will supply the lumber. But I need it in one week."

Santiago shook hands. "Sí Dios Quere," he said. To Melchor that meant, God willing. To Santiago, who as a boy had heard his mother use this expression every time he asked her for anything, it had a slightly different meaning. To him it meant: We'll see. Eventually he understood that it was her way of avoiding having to say no when that was what she really meant. So, as Melchor walked away satisfied that another detail for the festival had been settled, Santiago had already turned his mind to other matters. The platform stage, he figured, could wait a few days.

In-school Suspension at Sam Houston High was held in the old shop. This was nothing more than a tin-roofed garage with a cement floor and a couple of dozen battered desks sandwiched in between an ancient printing press, a broken lathe, and rows of disused lockers. There was no AC. A pair of enormous floor fans roared at the back of the room and blew away everything that wasn't nailed down, including the dog-eared pages the students were supposed to copy as part of their punishment. These pages had titles like "Respect for Authority" or "Following School Policy" or "Conflict Resolution." Each student was handed a sheet upon entering ISS and the idea was that the text addressed the transgression the student had committed. In practice, it rarely worked that way. Usually, the ISS teacher just handed the pages out randomly, four or five to each student.

Upon entering ISS that morning, Danny had been handed four sheets, none of which had anything to do with the reason he'd been sent there. He had been assigned two days of ISS for calling Mrs. Webb a "dried-out cunt" in the clear hearing of the Vice Principal. Danny's only defense was that the name was not undeserved, and he suggested a pelvic exam of the woman in question might exonerate him. The second remark earned him the second day.

The teacher assigned to ISS was a gray-haired man named Jones, who was sitting at his desk, drinking coffee and eating donuts out of a paper bag. He had notoriously bad breath but the students liked him because he paid no attention to them at all. He spent most of his time playing solitaire.

Danny nodded to two of the boys, regulars like him, and took a seat near the back. He took a few sheets of paper from his backpack and started to copy the pages. The only rule Mr. Jones enforced was that you had to copy at least four pages before the end of the day, and Danny liked to get his done early so he could draw or talk to his friends. He was about to finish copying his first page, "Listening is Learning," when he heard the heavy metal door behind him open. He turned and was surprised to see Flora Escalante walk into the room.

Girls like Flora never got sent to ISS so Danny assumed she was running an errand, perhaps bringing work from one of the teachers who still followed the policy of keeping ISS students involved in the curriculum. Mr. Jones obviously made the same assumption.

"Can I help you?" he asked, brushing the crumbs from the front of his shirt. Danny smiled. Flora had that effect on teachers.

Flora didn't answer the question. She handed Mr. Jones the blue ISS slip and asked, "Where do I sit?" Mr. Jones stared at the slip as though he'd forgotten how to read.

"Anywhere, anywhere," he said, putting the blue slip on his desk where he continued to stare at it. Finally, he shrugged and took out another donut. He was so disconcerted by Flora's arrival he'd forgotten to give her pages to copy. Flora exhaled sharply and turned on her heel. She was not going to be a happy camper, Danny thought.

Flora took one look at who was in ISS that day and blanched. First of all, she was the only girl present. Secondly, three of the boys had asked her out in the last month, and all been turned down. She was almost relieved, therefore, to see Danny at the back of the room.

She slid between the desks, ignoring the eyes that followed her, and took a seat beside him.

"What the hell are you doing here?" Danny said loudly. It was impossible to whisper with those fans bellowing, but Mr. Jones was hard of hearing anyway.

"Tardies," said Flora. "I have six tardies."

"They give you ISS for that?" said Danny incredulously. He was tardy so often he had an easier time counting the classes he's arrived to on time. That number would be zero, he figured.

"What are we supposed to do?" asked Flora. "Just sit here?"

"Nah. You're supposed to copy these pages. Teachers are supposed to send work, too, so we don't miss out on instruction. They never do, though."

"How did you get here?"

"Me?" Danny tried his best to look innocent, which only made him look silly. Flora laughed. "I was framed," he said.

"Yeah, I figured."

"Truth is, I have a standing reservation every Thursday, and sometimes on Friday, too." He leaned closer and lowered his voice. "This place is a well-kept secret, so don't go blabbin' about it or everyone will want to come." Flora laughed again. "I've known some kids to get in trouble just so they can spend a day here. It's the peace and quiet, I suspect."

"Well, that would be me then," said Flora. "I needed a vacation from school work."

"Sure. You came to the right place. And," he said, wiping the sweat from his forehead, "we have a built-in sauna."

Danny knew he was being a clown, and he always hated boys that did that just to impress girls, but he couldn't help it. He had seen Flora laugh and smile, and now all he wanted to do was see the white of her teeth or watch her breasts shudder as she laughed. He grinned at the other boys and they threw imaginary knives into his chest.

Flora had never seen Danny act this way before. She had always thought of him as one of the nerds, but now he seemed, well, almost nice.

"So, why are you tardy so much?" Danny asked.

"It's Mr. Rigby's class. I hate him. He's *such* a pervert!" This last word was said so loudly that several of the boys laughed. Mr. Jones looked up from his deck of cards suspiciously. Teachers, Danny knew, hated to hear kids laugh. They always assumed you were laughing at them, which was rarely the case.

"Why's he a pervert?"

"You know why he sits on that little stool in front of the lab table? So he can look up your skirt."

"Well, I don't usually wear skirts to school."

Flora slapped his arm playfully. Danny blushed. "I'm sure we're all happy about that, Danny."

He could not recall if she'd ever said his name out loud before, and the sound of it coming from her made him surprisingly happy. He had always considered Flora beautiful, but he had dismissed her as part of the "in" crowd on campus, and therefore unattainable to a "nerd" such as himself. But now, sitting beside her and looking at the way the fans blew her hair into her face, the way she brushed it away with a gesture of such off-handed grace, he began to entertain the thought that perhaps she was not so unattainable after all.

They spent the rest of the morning talking. When the lunch trays arrived they ate together. By this time, the other boys in the class had begun to misbehave in an effort to draw Flora's attention away from Danny. Mr. Jones put up with a lot, but when Raul Torres tossed a pickle into the fan, he called an administrator.

Mr. Russell, the assistant principal, arrived breathlessly. He took one look around the room and called Mr. Jones aside. A moment later, he asked Raul to leave the room. Like a gladiator who knows his fate is sealed, Raul had nothing to lose. He refused to get up. When Mr. Russell insisted, he shot him the finger.

A small, pear-shaped man with an enormous bald spot, Mr. Russell was no match for Raul, who was nearly six feet tall and weighed over two hundred pounds. He sized up the situation quickly and got on the radio, calling for the campus cop to come and remove Raul.

Flora, who had never seen such an incident before, was visibly nervous. Danny leaned over and said as quietly as possible, "He's just being an asshole to try to impress you." But the remark was not quiet enough, and Raul shot out of his seat and went for Danny.

"Fuck you, motherfucker!" he yelled.

Danny jumped out of his seat and pushed it toward Raul, who crashed into it and cursed even more loudly. Mr. Russell tried to interpose himself between the two students but slipped on the lunch tray that Danny had knocked over when he shoved the desk. Raul, having negotiated the desk, now fell over Mr. Russell. Danny grabbed Flora by the arm and pulled her behind the printing press. Mr. Jones joined the melée but only managed to step on Raul's arm. Raul, by then hopelessly interlocked with Mr. Russell, grabbed Mr. Jones by the leg and bit him. Mr. Jones screamed and collapsed on top of the heap. At this point, the campus cop entered the room, took one look at the situation, pulled out his pepper spray, aimed at Raul, and pressed the nozzle. The pepper spray, caught in the enormous wind generated by the floor fans, flew right back in the officer's face. He fell to the floor writhing in pain. Several boys who'd been standing behind him caught some of the spray, too. Soon the entire room was filled with the sounds of screams.

Ten minutes later, the fracas was over. Raul was led away by Mr. Russell and Mr. Jones, who was limping badly. The other students were in the nurse's office, along with the campus cop. Danny and Flora, the only unscathed members of the party, sat on the steps outside the ISS room and watched the parade of the injured as they departed. Mr. Holcombe, the principal, watched along with them, his hands on his hips, shaking his head.

"Danny Montez," he said, "I pray to God you had no hand in any of this."

"I didn't do anything," Danny protested. "He just went crazy"

Mr. Holcombe looked at him skeptically.

"It's true," Flora insisted. "You can ask Mr. Jones."

Mr. Holcombe shook his head. Flora, he knew, was a more than reliable witness. "Okay, okay. You two just sit here while I find someone to take over in there."

Danny and Flora did as they were told. After a while it became apparent that they'd been completely forgotten, so they got up and walked over to the football field. They sat together on the home bleachers, which were somewhat shaded by two Mesquite trees. The visitor's bleachers caught the full brunt of the sun.

Across the field, they watched Santiago carefully pruning the oleanders that grew around the base of the memorial scoreboard. He spotted them and they waved. He waved back and continued working.

Looking out across the green field, Flora sighed. "I wish all of Espantosa was this beautiful," she said wistfully. Danny nodded in agreement.

They sat in silence for a while, and then Danny slowly reached for her hand. She looked at him and smiled.

Santiago looked back over his shoulder only once. He saw the two figures on the bleachers lean toward each other, then he looked away, remembering a time long ago when he, too, had stolen a kiss on those same bleachers. The thought of that kiss, and what happened afterwards, filled him with happiness to this day. He was pleased to note, as his shears snipped at the long branches, that this memory could still provide him with an erection.

Chapter Ten

Though the old offices of the Espantosa Hourly Gazette were working out fine, there was one drawback. At first, Melchor thought the presence of the enormous press bothered only him, but when he spoke to Connie about his feelings he found she, too, was aware of its brooding presence.

"It's like some kind of behemoth," he told her. "And I can't help feeling that it's watching us."

Connie agreed. "Almost like it's waiting for something."

"My grandfather used to say 'A hammer is only happy when it meets the nail.'"

"Uh huh."

"But then he called his hammer Oscar," Melchor laughed.

"You're joking."

"No. If he dropped it on the ground, he'd say something like, 'Oscar, get back up here.' Or if he hit himself on the thumb, he say, 'Oscar, watch what you're doing.'"

"Your grandfather was something, huh? Did the hammer ever talk back to him?"

"Not that I know of," he chuckled. He leaned over and put his ear against the press. "Sshh," he said. He closed his eyes and listened. "You know what?"

"You aren't going to tell me you can hear anything." Connie felt a nervous shudder run up and down her back.

"Yup." Melchor straightened up. "It says, 'I'm hungry.'"

Connie laughed and threw a paper cup at him.

"The strange thing about that hammer," he said, sitting down on a three-legged stool across from her, "is that when my grandfather died it showed up in his coffin, but no one would admit putting it there."

"Maybe when Umberto passes away, he should be buried with his press. Like that woman in California who was buried inside her Cadillac."

"Have to be a pretty deep hole."

Connie walked over to the press. "You know, maybe this thing *is* trying to tell us something. Maybe we could put it to use."

"I don't see how."

"We can run off fliers, maybe even do some kind of festival program."

"That's a great idea, but there's one snag. I have no idea how to operate the thing."

Connie was undeterred. "It can't be that hard," she said.

"You know, I just remembered, Umberto had a name for his press, too."

"What did he call it?"

"El Diablo."

Miss Coakely pulled up in front of the Gazette offices and turned off her motor. She had been attempting to run into Melchor Mendoza for the better part of the day. Though she knew a casual encounter was best for her purposes, in the end she had been forced to track him down. With a sigh, she got out of the car, the Book tucked under her arm.

Mendoza looked up when she entered and smiled. He walked over to her and extended his hand.

"I didn't know Espantosa had a newspaper," Miss Coakely said, opening the Book.

"It doesn't. At least not any more. We're just using the office space for the festival."

Miss Coakely made a note in the Book. "What was the name of the paper?"

"The Hourly Gazette. I hope you're still planning to stay for the festival."

"I'm not paid to vacation, Mr. Mendoza. I have to move on soon."

"Really?"

Miss Coakely paused to let the idea sink in. "If I spend too much time in one place, my employers will withhold my check."

Mendoza shifted his weight uneasily and licked his lips. "I don't suppose," he offered nervously, "that we could make it easier for you. Maybe help out with expenses?"

"That would be highly unethical."

"Yeah, I guess so."

At that moment, Connie emerged from behind the press, wiping gobs of ink from her hands. Miss Coakely, who thought Melchor was alone, quickly sized up the situation and realized the moment was not propitious. Though she had not had time to assess the threat Connie posed, she could not afford to let the conversation die now. "I could get fired for even having this discussion."

"I understand."

"And just who would do that?" asked Connie.

"My employer."

"I don't think I ever caught the name of your employer."

"I'm not supposed to tell people," Miss Coakely said thinly.

Connie glared at her. "Now why is that?"

Melchor stepped between the two women. "Maybe we should just focus on the festival for now," he said. He gave Connie a pleading look over his shoulder. "I'm sure we can come to an arrangement of some kind."

Miss Coakely's eyes were fixed on Connie. Her face was flushed, but she slowly mastered herself. She had to find some way to salvage the moment. "I don't see how," she said.

"Give me some time," Melchor said. "Stick around for a day or so and let me see what I can come up with."

"Suit yourself," said Miss Coakely. She closed her book and turned on her heel.

As she drove away, she pounded the dash with her fists. "Fuck!" she cried. She felt that she had staved off disaster, but barely. If only she had seen that Melchor was not alone! She would never have broached the subject. She had played her hand and now all she could do was sit back and wait. Patience was not her strong suit.

"Christ, don't tell me you're thinking of giving that girl money, Melchor!" Connie said fiercely. "I said I'd help and I will, but not if you're gonna make a fool of yourself over a little tramp with a black book."

"I don't care about Miss Coakely," Melchor protested. "I just want her to stay long enough to see the festival so it can go in the Book."

Connie looked at him long and hard. She realized it wasn't that he was making a fool of himself that irritated her, but something else. She groped in her mind to identify that

104

something. Then it struck her, and she almost laughed out loud such a surprise it was when she found it. She was jealous. This seemed so improbable as almost to be unimaginable, but there it was.

At the same time, Melchor perceived the source of her rage, and it astonished him even more than it did Connie. It was true he found Miss Coakely strangely attractive, but he had done nothing that could make Connie jealous. It was also quite clear that Miss Coakely was completely uninterested in him. Even though he was certain Connie's feelings were unwarranted, it gave him a deep thrill to realize he'd aroused such emotions in her. "I promise you," he said, suppressing a smile, "all I'm interested in is the Book."

"Fine," she said at last. "But you are *not* going to give that woman money."

Melchor opened his hands helplessly. "I don't see how I can avoid it."

"Trust me," said Connie. "That girl is not going anywhere."

Oscar Escalante, husband of Olga, son of Maria, father of Flora and Rosa, often told people he must have been cursed as a child. How else, he would ask, could you explain the fact that his life came to be so dominated by women?

"To have one daughter is a blessing," he would say. "To have two daughters is a blessing." He held up two fingers to illustrate the point. "To be married to a beautiful woman is a blessing." He extended another finger. "To have a saint of a mother is another blessing," he added, raising another finger. "To live with all of them in the same house, that is a curse!" He emphasized the point by punching the air with his thumb.

On this particular afternoon, the curse seemed to have come home to roost. Maria had fallen last week and though she had not been seriously injured, she did suffer a badly sprained ankle and some ugly bruises. Because of her injuries, she refused to leave her bedroom.

Olga had been waiting on her for the past five days, and the strain was beginning to show. Oscar had given his mother a small bell to ring when she needed anything, but she was so impatient that she would begin to pound on the wall with her cane if no one answered the summons instantly.

Oscar, lying on the sofa watching ESPN, heard the tinkling of the bell and called to his wife. Before she could answer, the old woman began to pound on the wall.

"AY!" Olga exclaimed from the kitchen. "I'm going to break that cane in half!"

Oscar grabbed the remote and turned up the TV.

"How is her ankle going to get any better if she doesn't start walking on it?" Olga passed through the living room carrying Maria's lunch and a glass of chocolate milk. Maria had developed a sweet tooth in recent months.

"Dad!" Oscar turned up the TV some more. "Dad!"

A moment later, Rosa, his youngest daughter was standing before him, her hand on her hips, glaring at him. How, Oscar thought, did young girls learn so quickly how to look at men like that? "I was calling you!" Rosa complained. "Flora took my eye shadow!"

At twelve, Rosa was just beginning to wear makeup. Oscar did not approve of this development, but Olga argued that if she didn't have her own she was just going to use her friends'. Still, he could not get used to seeing his youngest daughter with lipstick and eye shadow. He thought she looked much nicer without makeup, anyway. He was proud that his daughters were pretty, but he worried that they would make bad choices. Just yesterday, he had seen Flora walking home with the Montez boy. Oscar had never liked Danny, and he certainly did not like his bitch of a mother. He much preferred the Cade boy to Danny, and he intended to let Flora know this.

"Go get your mother," Oscar said, motioning for her to move aside. "I'm watching TV."

Olga appeared at that moment. "Oscar! I have my hands full. Can't you handle this?" She glared at him. Oscar looked back and forth at his wife and his daughter and decided the origins of that look were not so mysterious after all.

He got to his feet and walked heavily down the hall with Rosa in tow. He turned sharply and said, "Goddammit, I'm gonna take care of it. Now go help your mother."

Rosa turned on her heel and walked off in a huff.

Oscar knocked on Flora's door. His oldest daughter had become sensitive about her privacy ever since Oscar walked in on her while she was in her bra and panties. Flora, horrified, had screamed for her mother.

Oscar, who often walked around the house in his underwear, couldn't understand what all the fuss was about.

"I changed your diapers and wiped your ass, for Chrissake!" This only prompted a groan from Flora.

"It's different," Olga explained. "Flora is becoming a woman."

Oscar had a hard time grasping this, but in the end he acquiesced, and so he dutifully knocked on his daughters door and waited, submissive as an ox.

There was no response. He heard Olga's voice rising sharply in the kitchen followed by the sound of Rosa whining. He knocked again.

He opened the door and peered cautiously inside. Flora was lying on her bed, her walkman beside her. Her eyes were closed and her lips were moving soundlessly. Olga was right, Oscar reflected, as he looked at his daughter's full bosom, her long, shapely legs— she was becoming a woman. This realization filled him with dread. What kind of yahoo, he wondered, was she going to get hitched up with in a town like this? Not, on his life, Danny Montez.

Flora sensed his presence and opened her eyes. She removed the headphones and Oscar could hear the thin, tinny sound of music. Too loud, he thought, too loud.

"I knocked," he said apologetically.

"That's fine. What's up, Daddy?"

"Uh," Oscar tried to shift gears, "your sister says you have her makeup."

"What makeup?"

Oscar was stumped. "I don't know. Makeup."

"I have her eyeshadow." She pointed to her dresser. Oscar saw a thin black plastic case. He picked it up and sat down on the bed.

"I've been wanting to talk to you," he began. Flora smiled, but he felt her tense ever so slightly. "Yesterday, the Montez boy walked you home."

"Danny," Flora said helpfully.

"Yeah." Oscar paused. Flora looked at him blankly. It was always her strategy when confronted by her parents to admit nothing but the simple truth and deny any implications. It had served her well and she was not about to abandon it now. Oscar, on the other hand, operated under the prejudice that as the parent he was naturally entitled to know everything about his child's life. At the same time, he hated to pry. Faced with Flora's blank stare, he used the only weapon at his disposal: uncomfortable silence. He waited.

Flora smiled at him and began to study the polish on her fingernails. Oscar smoothed the comforter, sighed, and began to pry.

"So," he said quietly, "are you two an item?"

Flora reacted as though he'd dropped a live rattlesnake in her lap. She jumped off the bed and shouted, "Why do you always have to do this? Can't I have a private life?"

Oscar stood up and faced her. The simple answer, he knew, was no. He decided against the simple answer. "Flora," he began, "but that boy, he's just no damn good."

"You don't even know him."

This was untrue, but Oscar realized he was not going to get anywhere by pointing out the obvious. Two years ago, Danny and two other boys had been caught trying to steal the stereo out of Oscar's pickup. Mrs. Montez had appealed to Oscar to no avail. She then spoke to Olga, who was moved to ask Oscar to drop the charges. He regretted it to this day.

"I don't want you to spend time with that boy," he said, his own voice rising.

"You just want to run my life!"

Olga, who had heard the ruckus in the kitchen, came into the room at this point. "What is going on?" she said, and looked at both of them accusingly. Oscar was offended by that look, as though he and Flora were siblings caught arguing rather than father and daughter.

"I want my eye shadow," said Rosa, who had followed her mother.

"Do you have her eye shadow?" Flora pointed to her father. He handed Olga the case. "Oscar, I ask you to handle one simple thing. Do you think I need this right now?"

Before Oscar could respond, the doorbell rang. "I'll get it," he said quickly, grateful for the chance to leave the room.

As he walked toward the front door, he heard his mother's cane pounding on the wall. For a moment, he stood still in the middle of the living room, considering whether he should just slip out the back door.

With a sigh, he opened the door. Almost immediately, he realized he should have run when he had the chance.

It was Melchor Mendoza.

Melchor was Oscar's second cousin. The two men, only three months apart in age, had grown up together. Though their families gathered often, the two of them never got along. Oscar, scrappy and tough, disliked his quiet, shy cousin. He took every opportunity to make fun of Melchor, pushing him to play sports, at which Melchor was completely hopeless. Their games were invariably one-sided. Oscar had a seemingly endless appetite for crushing his cousin, and Melchor quietly obliged him, smiling good-naturedly every time his cousin won a basketball game or knocked him to the ground at football. That Melchor never seemed to mind losing only increased Oscar's dislike for the boy.

At school, Melchor excelled, while Oscar was held back in the third and fifth grades. By the time he got to middle school, Melchor was already two grades ahead of him. As his grades continued to spiral downward, Oscar's mother thought he would benefit from tutoring. To Oscar's utter shame, she asked Melchor.

Their tutoring sessions quickly dissolved into games of one sort or another. More often than not, they wound up outside shooting baskets on the rusted hoop Oscar's father had hung from a pole over a sandy patch of ground. Oscar was particularly vicious in these games, and more than a few times Melchor went home from these "tutoring sessions" with skinned knees or a bloody nose. Melchor never complained. He seemed to sense that Oscar's fierce competitiveness was rooted in something else besides his dislike for him. After a few short weeks, when Oscar's grades failed to improve, the tutoring was discontinued.

In the last week of his 6th grade year, Oscar was called to the counselor's office. There he was told that he would again be retained if he did not attend summer school. The counselor went on to say that he had already spoken to his mother and they had agreed that Oscar needed tutoring.

"Who's gonna tutor me?" Oscar asked, sure that he already knew the answer.

"Your cousin Melchor," the counselor told him brightly. He seemed to think Oscar would be happy to hear this news. "And I wouldn't worry so much," he added. "I'm sure with your cousin's help you'll be able to pass summer school and move up with your friends next year."

Oscar nodded glumly. He didn't bother to tell the counselor that next year all his friends would be in high school. The thought of being tutored by Melchor again filled him with dread.

After leaving the counselor's office, Oscar walked slowly back to class. As he approached the sixth grade hall, he saw Melchor, who was an office aide, approaching from the opposite direction. Melchor looked up at him and smiled. Oscar lowered his head and walked on. Melchor, sensing something was wrong, made the mistake of asking Oscar what had happened.

A few minutes later, several teachers burst from their doorways, drawn by Melchor's high-pitched screams for help. They found Oscar on top of him, pummeling his fists into Melchor's bloody face.

Oscar finished out the school year at home. He did not attend summer school. His only consolation was that he did not see Melchor for a long, long time.

By the time Oscar entered high school, Melchor was a senior. The two boys had little contact. It was not until Melchor had graduated and Oscar had dropped out that they met up again. This time, it was at a technical school in San Antonio. Though Melchor had had good grades in high school, he was already beginning to show signs of his later political activism. He had several run-ins with the administration over policies he considered unfair, such as the preferential treatment of athletes and the use of politically incorrect textbooks. In particular, his attempt to have banned *Texas History Movies*, a comic that depicted Anglo expansionism as heroic destiny, sent him afoul of the school board. Melchor argued one passage in the comic was particularly offensive. It depicted Mexican soldiers on their knees as tears poured from their eyes, exclaiming, "Me no Alamo! Me no Goliad!" When it came time for scholarships to be awarded, Melchor found that he had not been recommended for a single one. His mother was deeply disappointed, but his father seemed relieved.

"Best thing for him," he said. "Now he can go and learn a trade." Melchor was sent to live with his aunt in San Antonio.

At technical school, the tables were turned. Oscar, who had passed his GED with great difficulty, excelled in the hands-on program. Melchor, defeated and dejected, managed to last only six weeks. The result was that Oscar left the school as a qualified electrician and Melchor returned to Espantosa with no prospects for a job and no hope of attending college.

Oscar's success had the effect of tempering his hatred of his cousin. Over the years, he had quite forgotten about the abuses he'd heaped on him, and though he never came to like him, Oscar could at least tolerate having Melchor live in the same town.

That didn't mean he wanted Melchor showing up on his doorstep.

"What can I do for you, Melchor?" Oscar made a point of blocking the doorway.

"I need to talk to you about something," Melchor said. "In fact, I need your help."

"Your electricity go out or what?"

"No, no. Nothing like that." Melchor looked past his cousin and waved to Olga who had come to see who was at the door.

The instincts of a politician are not so far removed from those of a salesman. Melchor was enough of a politician to realize quick action was called for. He put his foot in the door. "Actually," he said quickly, "it's about your bike."

Oscar looked at him doubtfully. "My bike?"

"Can I come in and explain?"

"What the festival needs is attractions," said Melchor. He was sitting on the sofa in the Escalante living room. He had a glass of tea in his hand and as he spoke, he rattled the ice gently.

"Would you like some more tea?" Olga asked.

114

"I'd love some more. Best tea I ever had. It's so..." Melchor paused. Olga, bending over to take his glass, paused too. "So cold!" Melchor said at last. Olga smiled and took his glass. "Now, where was I?"

"You were talking about attractions," said Oscar. He heard the sound of a bell from the back of the house, followed immediately by the cane pounding. He saw Olga in the kitchen throw up her hands. She came back and handed Melchor his glass and left, but not without throwing Oscar an angry look.

"Yes, yes. Well, we have plenty of concessions and we don't need more of those. But people like to wander around in a festival, and we got nothin' for them to wander around to." He took another sip of tea and looked at the glass judiciously. "Very nice glass. Where did you get these?"

"Wal-Mart. I still don't see how this connects to..."

"I was coming to that. I was lying awake last night when it suddenly hit me. You know lots of bikers, so why not ask them to come to Espantosa? What is the name of that club, the one in Crystal City?"

"The Road Hogs."

"The Road Hogs. Do you think you could arrange to have them come here?"

"And do what? Stunts or something?" Ever since Oscar had used his entire income tax rebate to put a down payment on a second hand 1982 Road King (a purchase of such extravagance that it nearly caused Olga to sue for divorce), he had been a member of the Road Hogs. Oscar could not imagine the aging bikers he rode with on the weekends jumping over flaming barrels or performing acrobatic twists above the heads of an amazed audience.

"No, nothing like that. I just want them to come and show off their motorcycles."

"You mean like in a parade?"

"No. I just want you to ask your buddies to bring their motorcycles out to the football field."

"You talk to Santiago about that?"

"He doesn't own the field."

"It's got his fuckin' name on it."

"Listen," said Melchor, "I'll take care of the football field. But tell me, honestly, can't you just see them, all those brightly polished machines gleaming in the sunlight against that green, green field?"

Yes, Oscar could.

Chapter Eleven

"I do think tea is a civilizing influence, don't you, Miss Coakely?" said Mrs. Gill. The three of them, Mrs. Gill, the Pastor, and Miss Coakely, were sitting on the front porch of the Gill home. A chipped tea set with mismatched cups sat on the rusty, wrought iron table in front of them. Mrs. Gill began to pour.

"Lemon?" she asked.

"Yes, please," said Miss Coakely. It was a mystery to the Pastor, but the only person the girl seemed to treat decently was his wife. It bothered him to no end.

"I'm sure you have an opinion on this matter, do you not, young lady?"

"On what matter?" said the girl, slurping her tea.

"On tea as a civilizin' influence, of course."

"Tea is tea," she said.

"Oh, dear, just imagine the world without tea. Why there would never have been a British empire without tea!" Mrs. Gill was a big fan of the British empire. She seemed not to know it no longer existed, having formed her impression of it chiefly through British television shows she watched on public broadcasting.

"The British empire subjugated and abused millions of people all over the world," said Miss Coakely.

"Oh, of course they didn't. That's just propa... propa... what is called, Mr. Gill?"

"Propaganda," said the Pastor.

"Yes, of course," said Mrs. Gill. "That's just propaganda. Oh, my dear, what lovely hands you have!"

"Miss Coakely does not agree," said the Pastor. He could not tolerate his wife's refusal to admit the tension Miss Coakely had brought into their home so he was constantly stoking the flames, but to no avail.

"I used to have pretty hands, didn't I, Mr. Gill? But I've washed too many dishes in my life, you see. Not that I'm complaining, of course."

"I think your hands are lovely, dear," said the Pastor, planting a kiss on her pudgy knuckles.

"Oh, you'll make me blush, Mr. Gill," said Mrs. Gill, and as proof, she did blush. Then she put her hand to her mouth and gasped. "Good gracious, the cookies!" She rushed back into the house.

Pastor Gill turned to the girl. "I think this has gone on long enough, little sister," he said.

"What are you talking about?" said the girl over the top of her teacup.

"This little joke of yours isn't funny. I want you out of my house."

"What little joke?"

"You're playing my wife for a fool."

"As far as I can see, Mr. Gill, the only fool here is you."

The Pastor stood up. "I want you out! Do you hear me?" he said sharply.

"I think your wife will have something to say about that," Miss Coakely said pleasantly.

"These are chocolate mint!" said Mrs. Gill, arriving on the porch, bearing the tray of cookies. She looked at the Pastor. "What's happened here?" she said.

"Miss Coakely was just telling me she has to leave," said the Pastor thickly.

"Oh, nonsense," said Mrs. Gill, laying the tray on the table and upsetting the tea cups. "She told me just this morning she'll be with us for a few more days, didn't you, Miss Coakely?"

"That's right, Mrs. Gill," said the girl, leaning back in her chair and biting into a cookie. "I haven't finished my research."

"There then, it's all settled. Now, dear," she said, "You must try one of these. They are simply delicious."

"Her research is over," said the Pastor.

"Don't be difficult, Mr. Gill, you just heard her say she has more to do. I'm sure she wouldn't dream of missing the festival. I think we are so lucky to have you, my dear," she said, turning to Miss Coakely and laying her hand on her arm.

"Thank you, Mrs. Gill," said Miss Coakely. She looked up at the Pastor with insolent satisfaction.

Pastor Gill turned and walked inside, his hands clenched. He let the screen door slam shut behind him.

"Don't mind him, my dear," said Mrs. Gill. "You are welcome in our home as long as you want to stay. Such pretty hands," she said again, taking one of Miss Coakely's hands in her own and stroking it. "I used to have pretty hands, you know."

The pastor walked furiously into the bathroom and shut the door behind him. He stood in front of the sink and gripped the basin with both hands. Over the long years of his ministry, he had faced many challenges, but never had he felt so wretchedly helpless.

119

He had been unfaithful many times over the course of his twenty year marriage. There had been tears, recriminations, and threats of divorce, but he had weathered it all. In those cases, his wife had reacted with such rage that on more than one occasion, he feared for her sanity and his safety. All of this had been a long time ago, and since their move to Espantosa, the Pastor had been the model of fidelity. Even now, he had *done* nothing, but he knew this was not the whole story. The truth was, he desired Miss Coakely in a way he had not desired a woman in years. And he was sure his wife knew this. What he could not understand was her reaction to these circumstances. Not only did she not confront him, but she insisted that the source of these troubles remain in the same house. Far from being upset with him, she was nothing but sweetness and light.

He turned on the tap and ran his hands under the cool water. He washed his face. He was still, at nearly fifty, a handsome man. He had kept his looks and stayed trim, unlike his wife. He felt that letting herself go was a form of punishing him for the events that caused them to leave San Antonio, that set in motion their move (her idea) to Espantosa. At the time, he felt unable to oppose her, guilty as he was of the worst indiscretion. He had realized only recently how much he resented being forced into coming here. That the move saved his marriage there could be no doubt. That it also ended all hopes of a widespread ministry, also no doubt. But no. When he was honest with himself, he realized that he did not have the touch, that he could never have aspired to be much more than he was. There were times even when he felt that he had landed in the right place. Ultimately, he was where the Lord wanted him, and if his wife was the instrument of this, so be it.

He was no longer angry with his wife. He was almost surprised, in fact, to realize how much he still loved her. It only made him feel worse for desiring another woman, especially *that* woman.

He dried his face. He felt calmer now. Let the girl stay, he decided. He wanted nothing more to do with her.

But even as he framed this thought, he felt deep within him the tender shoots of desire pushing their way up through the soil of regret.

Though nearly everyone in Espantosa was aware of Gorman's nocturnal hobby, few ever made a fuss about it. In a town as small as Espantosa any secret worth knowing was bound to come out sooner or later. Besides, Gorman was a great source of gossip, and gossip was always welcome in Espantosa. This tolerance was, however, rooted in more than mere open-mindedness. Gorman was the town's only plumber, and, more importantly, he owned the only septic pump in town. No one relished the idea of Gorman being behind bars when their toilets started to back up.

Recently, Gorman had noticed a pungent odor in his own bathroom. Since he had pumped his own tank a few weeks before, he was at a loss to explain the origin of the stench. Even more puzzling was the regularity of the odor. It seemed to occur late at night, usually around three o'clock. Sometimes the stench was so foul it drove him out of bed. To Gorman's seasoned nose, it smelled like nothing so much as someone having taken a monstrous dump.

Aside from the displeasure of living in a house that was filled with such a stench, Gorman felt professionally challenged by the mysterious smell. He resolved to stay up late one night and keep an eye on things. He laid a few blankets down in the hallway, propped open his bathroom door, and settled in for the night.

A few hours later, Gorman woke up and almost retched. The bathroom door was shut, but the hallway was filled with a stench so suffocating it made him dizzy. He got to his feet and teetered for a moment, then, pulling a handkerchief from his pocket and covering his mouth, he pushed open the bathroom door.

What Gorman Price saw made his mouth fall open. Sitting on his toilet was a tall man in a suit, his trousers bunched around his ankles, a white Stetson perched jauntily atop his head.

"Jesus Christ," said Gorman.

The figure looked over at him and winked. "Close. Mighty close."

Helen Blas was wide awake watching the home shopping network. She had no interest in the featured product, a set of plates decorated with the legends of baseball, but she preferred it to other late night cable fare. Also, it comforted her to think there were enough people awake at that hour to keep the avenues of commerce open. Since her accident, Helen had watched her nights slowly change into days. Her habit of sleeping in short snatches prompted Roy to call her his "pussycat," an endearment she detested.

Roy had phoned near midnight to tell her that the shipment had not yet arrived. Helen hated to be alone at night, but it did mean she could keep the volume turned up on the TV, not that she really needed to listen to what was being said.

The accident had not rendered sex impossible for Helen, but it was, more often than not, painful. Over the last couple of years, Roy had put on weight, and this made it even more difficult. Often Helen, under the weight of his burgeoning belly, had to plead for him to get it over with. As their sex life diminished, Helen noted a disturbing development. In recent years, Roy had become more and more childlike in his affections. No longer a sexual presence in her husband's life, Helen found herself increasingly and unwillingly playing the maternal role. She noted how often Roy sought her approval these days, and how easily hurt he was when she withheld it.

The featured product changed. It was now a set of pewter figurines from Germany that Helen found disturbingly phallic. The figurines were marked down from $299 to $99. Did anyone believe those original prices, she wondered? How stupid do they think people are? Pretty fucking stupid. The figurines were selling fast. Helen glanced at the clock. It was almost three. She wondered if the phallic aspect of the figurines was not what was being marketed after all. She watched the host run her finger along the edge of one of the figurines and smile. How many women, she wondered, alone in their beds as she was, reached for the phone without ever realizing what they really wanted was a good fuck?

She mused on the ubiquity of the phallic image, appearing everywhere from architecture to bottles of Mr. Clean. She recalled a psychology class she had taken in junior college, during her short-lived academic career. The prof had recounted how Freud had scandalized the psychological community by suggesting that the cigar was a phallic symbol. The class had laughed and the professor, holding up a pencil, said, "Of course, phallic symbols, just like the genuine article, come in all sizes." Yup, she thought, and even in pewter.

She considered calling the café again, but thought better of it. Her first thought, when she heard Roy was going to be out late, was that he would be meeting that waitress. In the general disdain with which Helen viewed the world, she reserved a special category for women like Connie. To her mind, anyone who remained single past the age of thirty was suspect. She turned off the television and tired to forget about those figurines and all they implied.

Melchor was awakened by the sound of air brakes. He rolled out of bed and padded over to the open window. On the street below, a large refrigerator truck had pulled up in front of the Tumbleweed Café. A moment later, Roy Blas came out to speak to the driver. He signed the chit and the driver went to the back of the truck and unstrapped a dolly. Melchor watched as he began to wheel in the boxes.

The testicles had arrived.

Chapter Twelve

The night her husband, in his pajamas and slippers, walked out of his house and into the storm, Maria Walsh was at the movies. She had driven to Carrizo Springs with a girlfriend to see *Angel Face* for the third time. She had always liked Robert Mitchum, but what she loved about the movie was the final scene. Each time she saw the look on Mitchum's face as Jean Simmons shoved the car into reverse, she felt an odd thrill. The sight of the convertible plunging into the canyon always made her gasp. Later, she would recall that it was just about that time when Tom stepped in front of the tanker. Though she was shocked and saddened by her husband's death, she could not help thinking what a fine ending it would have made in a movie.

In a strange way, she was proud of Tom. True, he had made a shambles of his life, but at least he had the courage to end it on his own terms. When she arrived home and saw the patrol car waiting in the rain, she knew Tom was dead.

"It's just like a movie," she told the state trooper, a pimply-faced kid in his early twenties. The trooper, at a loss, nodded and said, "Yes Ma'am."

It was a phrase she repeated several times over the next few days: "Just like the last scene of a movie." She replayed that scene in her head over and over. In her vision, she saw Tom standing beside the road, waiting for the oncoming lights, then stepping forward, his shoulders square, eyes open, looking death coldly in the face. The sky flashed, illuminating the oncoming tanker, and she wondered if, in that brief, incandescent moment, he realized it was his father's tanker. He would have smiled at that, admiring the irony.

What troubled Maria the most, beyond the simple fact of her husband's death, was that such a rare moment could only come at the end of the movie. Ever since she was a girl, Maria had wondered what happened to the characters once the picture was over. Wasn't that when the screen faded to black? She realized it was up to her to fill in the remainder of her life's story now, and she did not feel up to the task.

Whenever someone suggested to Tom Walsh, as they often did when he was younger, that he ought to be in pictures, he waved off the suggestion with a smile. He recognized that such a suggestion was really only an expression of envy, and he knew he was no one to be envied.

When he was in school, he was forced to read "Richard Cory" in front of his class. He considered this an act of sadism on the part of his teacher, a man who earned less in a year than Tom's father could spend in a single day. When he got to the last line, "Richard Cory went home and put a bullet in his head," his teacher actually applauded. The rest of the class, sensing there was something abnormal in this exchange between student and teacher, was silent. When his teacher asked, with undisguised relish, what Tom thought of the poem, he answered, "I think it's a piece of shit." That remark earned him a paddling.

The poem did have an effect on Tom, though perhaps not the one the teacher intended. Many nights after reading that poem, Tom lay awake in his bed certain that at any moment he would hear the sound of a gunshot reverberate through the enormous house. Often, he braced himself for this, holding his breath, his body tense, but it never came. The closest Wallace Walsh ever came to committing suicide was nearly a decade later, when he put a bullet not through his own head but through that of his prized bull. Suicide by proxy, Tom called it. Unless it was murder by proxy. Tom was never sure whose face his father might have imagined as he pulled the trigger, his own or that of his son?

When Maria left the house on the final night of his life, Tom barely noticed her departure. It was not merely that he was drunk, but rather that his wife had ceased to be a presence in his life. Though she had initially ranted and pleaded with him over his drinking, in the end she had quietly acquiesced, preferring to visit her sister or go out to the movies with a girlfriend than to stay at home and watch him drink himself to death.

Tom regretted having married Maria. He had come to Espantosa listless and depressed, looking for a place to get away from people. Though his first thought had been to escape his father's sphere of influence, he did not realize that he was also looking for someone. He sensed within himself the seed of destruction and he was looking for someone to save him because he felt unable to save himself.

So it was that on that calm summer evening when he walked through the streets of Espantosa and saw Maria approaching, he saw in her not only a pretty girl but the instrument of his salvation. Later, he would explain this to her, and she laughed and kissed him. For her part, she confessed, she thought he looked like a lost little boy.

Tom remembered that discussion as he sat at the kitchen table, listening to the rain and thunder, drinking whiskey and eating saltine crackers to settle his stomach. It had not been fair for him to expect Maria to save him. He had realized that early in their marriage. He knew now what he did not know then: he did not want to be saved. All he really wanted was to be left alone. Many times, Tom resolved to get into the car and leave, but he could not bear to add any more weight to his already overburdened conscience.

On that night, however, he felt that leaving Maria was perhaps the lesser of evils after all. He had been working out a plan in his mind for several weeks, and it seemed to him that the time was ripe for action. His plan was simple. He would leave Espantosa, and once on the road he would call his father, explain that he had left Maria, that he wanted no more to do with her. His father would accept this explanation willingly. He would have him arrange for the divorce, and he would make sure Maria was provided for. He would tell his father he needed time to collect himself before coming home. Then he would simply disappear. It was a good plan, he thought groggily.

He picked up the bottle and grabbed his wallet and keys from the table by the front door. He didn't bother to change. He didn't bother to pack. *He was too drunk to think clearly, and he didn't even realize he was still in his pajamas.*

When he got outside, he walked to the driveway and stopped. The car was gone. He stood in the rain, blinking, trying to imagine where he'd left the car. Then he remembered that Maria had driven to Carrizo Springs. For a moment, he was unsure how to proceed. Finally, he decided it was better to leave her the car anyway. He could hitchhike. He walked away from his house, feeling he was leaving behind one life for another.

He stumbled vaguely through town. His pajamas were soaked and his slippers soggy. The storm raged above him and he wondered idly whether he might not be struck by lightning. Gradually, he made his way out of town. Approaching the highway, he squinted through the driving rain, looking for an oncoming car.

As the sky flashed, Tom's mind flashed with images of his father, and his mother, who had died when he was nine, of Maria walking down the street on that summer night when he mistook her for the angel of his salvation, of his father's prize bull lying dead at his feet, of a whiskey glass teetering on the edge of a table, of dozens of motel rooms where he passed the nights, drunk, with and without female companionship, of a small boy he'd discovered crying in the restroom at school when he was seven. Tears began to scald Tom's eyes. Now he felt the cold, his pajamas sticking to his skin. He no longer thought of escape. All he wanted was to go home and go to bed. He began to walk forward, unsure of the way home, thinking only of Maria, of seeing her hands and touching her face, of lying beside her in their bed and holding her tenderly as he hadn't done in such a long time.

He never even saw the tanker.

Chapter Thirteen

With the festival only a few days away, Melchor Mendoza felt the need to settle his nerves. He had spent most of the day exhorting the Titan Football team, who were showing signs of fatigue, to continue their efforts to give Espantosa a facelift.

"It's third down," he told them, "and we got the ball. Let's not think about punting. We gotta keep the drive going."

The boys looked at him blankly. For a team that in the previous year had managed only six first downs, the word drive was as alien as touchdown or championship.

Melchor sighed. "Let's just take it one step at a time."

As the boys were slapping paint onto the old bowling alley, Bill French happened by and commented to Melchor, "Trying to make this town pretty is like trying to paint up an old whore and bring her home to Mamma. She ain't never gonna be nothin' but a tired old hag that's been fucked all her life."

By the end of the day, even Melchor's spirits were flagging. The Aussie Goat Farm was some distance from Espantosa, but that evening Melchor felt the need to walk. He left his house as the sun was beginning to set and began the long trek. For years he had visited the Goat Farm whenever he felt the need to clear his head or revive his spirits. He was never sure why he chose that particular location for such a purpose, but it might have been that the farm represented the brief moment in time when

Espantosa had teetered on the edge of prosperity.

When he reached the farm that evening, the sun had turned the sky into a blazing canvas. He pushed open the rusted gate and continued down the long driveway until he reached the hulk of the main building. Countless teenagers had their way with this structure over the decades since it was abandoned. Windows had been smashed and holes gouged in the walls large enough for a man to walk through. Rows of ramshackle pens extended into the gloom.

Melchor sat down on an overturned crate that still bore a faded image of Sammy the Smiling Goat. Sammy's maniacal grin had terrorized children in the surrounding area for almost two years before being replaced by a kangaroo named Rooney. Rooney, while having no relation to the actual product he represented, at least had the virtue of never being confused with la chupacabra.

Maybe the reason he liked coming to the goat farm was that no matter how low he'd sunk in his life, he had never hit rock bottom like Sandy Foster, the farm's founder. His father had told him what he was like when he first arrived in Espantosa: a short, well-built man with a handlebar moustache who always wore his cowboy hat cocked to one side. You could tell a lot, his father claimed, by the way a man wore his hat.

When Sandy Foster first told the residents of Espantosa he intended to build a goat farm, everyone thought he was crazy. When he told them he planned to milk the goats instead of slaughtering them, they were convinced. The only advantage they could see in having a goat farm for a neighbor was the easy availability of cabrito, a succulent dish relished by many Texans. But when Sandy brought in the milking machines and began hiring the locals to run them, attitudes changed. When the farm went into full production, people were surprised to find that goat's milk wasn't half bad. For a time, Sammy the Goat smiled from the shelves of refrigerators in almost every house, and many Espantosa toddlers were weaned on the product of the Aussie Goat Farm.

After the collapse of his business, Sandy Foster disappeared. Some said he went back to Australia. Some said he fled to Mexico to escape his debtors. There were even stories that spoke of a wild man who had been seen near the banks of the Espantosa. Melchor thought the truth was probably something far more mundane.

After Sandy left, the town began the downward spiral from which it had never recovered. For a time empty houses in Espantosa outnumbered those that were lived in and the town resembled a movie set waiting for a cast that would never arrive.

And through it all, Espantosa remained, like a rash that wouldn't go away.

As the stars brightened in the darkening sky, Melchor felt his confidence growing. In the whole improbable history of Espantosa, there was never a time when things went right for long. He figured the town was due. He might have been less confident if he had remembered a saying his grandfather had been fond of. "Remember, mijo," he would tell Melchor, "things are never so bad they can't get worse." Then he would hook his thumb in the general direction of his wife, and grin like a schoolboy, "Ask her!"

It was a matter of some contention among the people of Espantosa what it was that really had set Melchor on the road to being a life-long pain-in-the-ass fuck-up. The popular view was that he was simply too smart for his own good, but many people held that his troubles really began when he hooked up with Umberto Marconi.

Marconi was the editor, publisher, and sole correspondent for the *Espantosa Hourly Gazette,* which, despite its name, was published as the banner unabashedly declared, "When There's News Enough to Print." The paper appeared at irregular intervals, sometimes twice a week, but more often a period of a month or more would pass between issues. Umberto dismissed suggestions to re-title the newspaper, stating that he was on the job twenty-four hours a day and it wasn't his fault if nothing newsworthy happened.

Umberto was that breed of man not uncommon in small towns everywhere: the iconoclast. Some people claimed he only published *The Gazette* as a means of spreading his views, which most dismissed as socialist or commie or just plain wrong. It was true that the "Editor's Note" often accounted for the lion's share of the paper's content.

There were several theories as to why Umberto had left his native Italy. Some said he had killed a man in a brawl and was forced to flee to avoid a vendetta. Umberto never denied this story, but neither would he confirm it. It was known he had spent time in New York before moving to Texas. A few people held he had run afoul of the mob while working as a reporter in New York. Whatever the reason, Umberto had clearly been on the move for a long time before settling in Espantosa, for he was already an old man when he arrived.

On the morning Melchor Mendoza walked into the tiny offices of *The Gazette*, Umberto had just lost a tooth. It was only the latest in a catalogue of losses which included one lung, one kidney, a portion of lower intestine, and the hearing in his right ear. Umberto viewed this latest loss as just one more instance of his body rushing to the grave ahead of him.

When Melchor entered, Umberto was staring accusingly at his tooth. "Go on, you bastard," he said. "I want nothing more to do with you." He looked up at Melchor and grinned. "Have you ever heard the expression, I'm not half the man I used to be? Well, in my case, pretty soon that's going to be true." He got up and dropped the tooth into a drawer of his enormous desk where it fell with a pitiful plunk. "Now, what can I do for you?"

"I wanted to see about a job," said Melchor.

Umberto opened the drawer of a rusty file cabinet and reached into it. To Melchor's surprise, he pulled out a scrawny cat. "Do you hear that, Lafcadio? We have an acolyte."

Lafcadio was named after Lafcadio Hearn, Umberto's favorite author. Like his master, the old cat had seen better days. He looked like he had been on the losing end of a lot of fights. The tip of one ear was missing and his face bore old scars as well as a few fresh wounds. One eye was swollen shut and his tail waved listlessly in the air like the flag of some Napoleonic retreat.

"I can't pay you, of course," said Umberto. "Lafcadio eats up all my profit, literally." He nudged the cat affectionately. "Actually, he's the editor in chief."

"I don't need to be paid," said Melchor, then he added, "not right away. I just want to learn."

"Learn? Learn what?" Umberto puttered around the stove, apparently searching for something. "Newspaper men lead lives of discontent. That's a fancy way of saying we're never happy. What is it you want to do?"

"I want to work for a newspaper," said Melchor.

Umberto approached him and stared at him closely. "Why?"

Melchor thought for a moment. He could smell the coffee on Umberto's breath. He had the feeling that what he said would decide whether or not the man was willing to give him a try. He wanted to give him a good answer, the best answer possible. In the end, he shrugged, "I don't know."

"That, my young friend, is an honest answer. Stupid, but honest. I'll take an honest newsman over a clever one every time." And with that the matter seemed to be settled.

Every day after school, Melchor showed up at the newspaper office. At first, the work was not what he had hoped for. Though Umberto referred to him as a stringer, he spent most of his time cleaning up, though he was learning how to set type. Often he passed the time playing dominoes with Umberto.

Sometimes Umberto sent Melchor on assignments.

"Get the facts, the facts," he exhorted. "Talk to people."

Melchor tried to do as he was told, but his interviews were invariably dismal. He found himself drawn into conversations about everything under the sun, except what he had come to talk about. When he tried to explain that he was a reporter sent to get a story, reactions ranged from hilarity to hostility.

"Tell that commie bastard I don't want nothing to do with his newspaper."

"Hey, look! It's Jimmy Olsen. A goddamn Mexican Jimmy Olsen."

"I can't talk to you. I already sold my story to *The New York Times*. Exclusive."

"What's that wop up to, sending a dumbass like you to talk to me? Tell him to send his cat. I won't talk to no one else."

Through it all, Melchor tried his best to get the story. He would return from his investigations to *The Gazette* offices and painstakingly compose his copy, only to have Umberto take one look at it, cluck his tongue, and rewrite the entire story.

Occasionally he would take the initiative and try to come up with a story on his own, like the time he wrote about the poor quality of Espantosa's drinking water. He interviewed his science teacher and several local residents. Everyone agreed that the water was basically undrinkable. He considered it a scandal and thought that his article would bring about

137

needed change, but when he showed it to Umberto the old man winced.

"Everyone knows we got shitty water. Why you want to draw attention to it?"

"So that we can change it."

"How?"

Melchor was at a loss. He had not considered that. "Well, I guess we could install a water purifier, then...."

"You got any idea what that would cost?"

"No," Melchor admitted glumly.

"It's bad enough people have to live in this town without you go and remind them what a shithole it is."

The story never appeared in print.

Though Melchor learned little about the newspaper business during his brief tenure with Umberto, the old man did awaken in him an interest in politics. Often that winter, they would sit together with their feet propped on the potbelly stove and Umberto would read aloud from the works of Aristotle, Machiavelli, Adam Smith or Karl Marx. This was an altogether different education from the one Melchor received in Civics class.

It was clear, however, that the lesson Melchor took from these talks was not exactly the one Umberto had intended. When he announced to the old man that he wanted to run for political office one day, Umberto was aghast.

"What?" he sneered. "You want to become one of those bastards?"

"I'll be different," said Melchor quietly.

"That's what they all say." He put his hand on the boy's shoulder. "I like you, Melchor.

You're a lousy newspaper man, but I like you. I'm gonna give you a piece of advice. Don't go into politics. You're not built for it. For one thing, you're too idealistic. You want to change the world, but the world doesn't want to be changed. Sure, people bitch and moan, but the truth is the poor bastards like things the way they are. It's what they know. And another thing. You're ugly. I hate to say it, but you are. Ugly doesn't get votes. And last but not least, you're Mexican, and no one votes for Mexicans."

Melchor took all this in silently. The old man picked up Lafcadio and sat down, stroking the cat and staring at the floor.

"Maybe you're right," said Melchor quietly.

"Of course I'm right. You take my advice. You go into anything but politics you got a better chance to make something of yourself someday. And one more thing. Get out of this town. It's nothing but a shithole and that's all it's ever gonna be."

"But that's just the trouble," said Melchor, rising to his feet. "You say no one wants things to change but that's only 'cause they don't know no better. Where would we be if everyone was like that?"

"Right where we are," said the old man with the barest trace of a smile.

"You know what," said Melchor fiercely, pointing his finger at Umberto, "you're one of them. You write your newspaper and you say all these things and you talk about great men and how they changed the world, but in the end you're just like everybody else."

"End of lesson," said Umberto. He looked up at the boy. "Now, sit down and have a cup of coffee with a tired old man."

Melchor sat down and Umberto poured him a cup of coffee from the tin pot on the stove. "Just the same," he said "I'm going to try."

"Of course you are," said Umberto, sipping his coffee loudly. "And God help you."

Though Melchor continued to visit Umberto after that day, they spent most of their time playing dominoes. Umberto did not give him any more assignments, and indeed the paper began to appear less and less often. As the years passed, Umberto added the vision in his left eye to his catalogue of losses. He lost Lafcadio, too. The old tomcat curled up under the press one day and died. Umberto was unable to retrieve the body and it slowly decomposed, stinking up the place for weeks.

It was a decade later, and just a few weeks before Umberto finally admitted defeat and allowed himself to put into a nursing home in Carrizo Springs, that he ran off the final issue of the *Espantosa Hourly Gazette*. The headline read: Melchor Mendoza Elected by Landslide. It was, in fact, the only time in his long career as a newspaper man that Umberto ever knowingly departed from the truth, claiming that Melchor had "won the election by a landslide on a platform of sweeping reform."

As he approached the town in the dark, Melchor thought he heard footsteps behind him. He turned, half expecting to see the ghost of Sandy Foster or even Sammy the Goat. There

140

was only a dog, black and skinny, who stopped as Melchor stopped, and regarded him from a distance. Melchor searched his pockets but he had nothing to give him. He bent over and whistled softly. The dog took a few tentative steps forward, then backed up.

"What are you scared of, you little coward," Melchor said. "I promise I won't bite you if you don't bite me."

Espantosa was such a small town that not only did everybody know everybody else, they knew their animals as well. Melchor was quite sure he had never seen this dog before. His first thought was to curse the no-good-sonavabitch who dumped the animal here. People were always dumping unwanted animals in and around Espantosa. It was the opposite, actually. No one ever had a dog or cat in Espantosa that they considered a pet. Animals were animals. People had dogs as cheap alarms or so they could be alerted when Old Lady Dawson's goat had wandered onto their property. They kept cats because they ate mice, and woe to the cat that proved a poor mouser. A bitch that had puppies was allowed to nurse her brood only until the runts could be weeded out.

Melchor had never owned a dog. He had been raised around too many mutts to want one of his own. On the other hand, he was superstitious, and he felt that perhaps he had been wrong about the dog. Maybe it had not been dumped out in the middle of nowhere. The more he stood and thought about it, regarding the dog in the moonlight, the more he was convinced that the dog was an omen. Without giving the matter any further thought, he called out to the dog, "Come here, Sandy. Come here boy!"

Almost immediately, as if recognizing its name, the dog bounded forward. Melchor reached down and patted his head. Sandy licked his hand.

"Okay, boy," said Melchor. "You and me, we're gonna put this town right, eh?"

Sandy looked up at Melchor and wagged his stumpy tail.

Chapter Fourteen

When she heard her daughter-in-law bring in her morning coffee, Maria pretended to be asleep. She snored softly as she listened to Olga moving around the room, snooping as usual. When she heard the door close, she opened her eyes and reached for her coffee. It was hot and sweet. She put the coffee aside to cool and reached under the blankets for the handheld Yahtzee game Rosa had given her for Christmas. Though she professed that she had no interest in such things, the truth was she was hooked. She pressed the buttons and began to play, cursing under her breath every time she got a bad roll.

She heard footsteps in the hallway and quickly tucked the game under the covers again. She closed her eyes and feigned sleep once more.

"Mama," said Olga. "There's someone here to see you."

Maria opened her eyes and sat up slowly with a low moan that would have been the envy of Camille. "Who's there?" she said, rubbing her eyes.

"It's Guadalupe Lopez," a voice answered. "And stop pretending you were asleep."

"Come in, come in," Maria said, waving her hand weakly.

"And stop pretending you're dying, too." Guadalupe sat down on the side of the bed.

"I am dying," Maria said petulantly. "And so are you. We're just taking our time about it."

"Bullshit," said Guadalupe. "You're as strong as a mule, and just as pigheaded as I am."

143

Maria conceded the point with a brief smile. "Did my son send for you?" she asked.

Guadalupe rolled her eyes. "You think the whole world revolves around you? Nobody cares if you stay in this filthy bed until you rot." She smacked her lips loudly. "Of course, while you're getting your beauty sleep, that woman is taking over the whole house. One day you'll get sick of lying around and take a step outside and you won't even recognize the place."

Maria raised a hand to her forehead. "¡Ay, Dios mío!" she exclaimed. "What has she done?"

"For starters, she recovered your little footstool."

"The one with La Virgen in silver and gold?"

Guadalupe nodded. "It's brown now. A shitty brown."

"Ay!" Maria cried, crossing herself. "What else?"

"Then she painted your kitchen."

"Oh," Maria said quietly. "Well, that's not so bad. It needed painting."

"It's orange."

Maria gasped, "Orange?"

"Yes. Then she went to Carrizo Springs and bought some carpet pieces on sale."

"Oh no!"

"Yes, she covered your floors." Guadalupe paused to let the idea sink in.

"What," said Maria tensely, "did she do with my rugs?"

"You know the one with the portrait of Lucha Villa?" Maria nodded, bracing herself. "It's in the garage."

Maria emitted a soft moan. "And the other?"

"Oh you mean the portrait of JFK and Jackie?"

"Yes."

"It's on the front porch."

"Stop, please," Maria whimpered.

"But I haven't told you about your collection of decorative plates yet!"

"Tell me," said Maria, shutting her eyes.

"The Davy Crockett plate is under an aloe vera on the porch. I saw the Lyndon Johnson plate in the kitchen. The cat is eating off it, I think."

"What about," Maria struggled for air, "the Tony Orlando?"

"The one with Dawn or without?"

"Just Tony. With the pineapples around the edges."

"Oh, that one. I saw it sticking out from under the sofa. I think Oscar is using it as an ashtray."

Maria fainted.

When Oscar came home for lunch that day, he found Olga sitting on the front porch holding a plastic bag of ice against her shoulder.

"¿Que paso?" Oscar said. Olga glared at him. Then from inside the house he heard his mother cursing in Spanish. It sounded like she was redecorating the house with a sledgehammer.

"What the hell?"

"Your mother," said Olga through gritted teeth, "has lost her mind." She removed the ice pack to reveal a large purplish bruise. "She actually hit me, with that goddamn cane!"

Oscar felt his stomach tighten into a ball the size of a walnut. "Jesus," he gasped. He looked through the window and saw his mother shredding a piece of carpet with a butcher knife.

"Well," he said, sitting down heavily on the porch step, "at least she's up."

News of Maria's recovery spread through the town quickly. While many people held that the old woman had been faking it all along, some were inclined to accept another explanation.

"She was possessed!" said Juanita Torres. "Guadalupe drove the demons from her!"

She was recounting the story at Mrs. Nelson's hardware store. A small crowd had gathered to listen, including Mrs. Nelson, Fent Hurley, Dolores Cantu, Manuela Garcia, and Pastor Gill.

"There was nothing wrong with that woman except she was too lazy or too tired to do for herself anymore," said Pastor Gill.

"Really, Pastor," Dolores sneered, "I would think that a man of God would be less ignorant about the ways of the Devil."

Pastor Gill rolled his eyes. Dolores ignored him and turned back to her audience. "The first thing Guadalupe did was bathe her in a mixture of Holy water and goat urine." Mrs. Nelson gasped. "But that only made her break out in boils and pustules."

"What are pustules?" said Hurley.

"They're like boils."

"So she broke out in boils and something like boils," said Hurley, giving the Pastor a wink.

"Rosa wanted to take her to the hospital right then and there, but Guadalupe said no. She took out one of her powders and told Maria to

146

make a tea of anise and pepper and parsley. Then she mixed in the powder and made Maria drink it. That's when all Hell broke loose." Dolores lowered her voice and crossed herself. "She called on Satan to help her, and a crucifix on the wall burst into flames, right there and then."

"That's blasphemy!" said Pastor Gill. "And what's more, it's a lie. That old woman...."

"Now Pastor," said Hurley, "there's no cause to spoil a good story just cause it ain't true."

Dolores glared at both men and was on the verge of saying something when the door to the hardware store opened and Oscar Escalante walked in. He took one look at everybody and stopped cold. It was obvious he'd come into the middle of something, and he thought he could guess what the topic of conversation had been. He walked over to the counter and waited, his back to the others.

"What can I get you, Oscar?" said Mrs. Nelson, moving behind the counter.

"I need some wood glue," said Oscar. He took a piece of paper out of the pocket of his overalls. "And, um, some rubber cement, and, uh, some plaster. Upholstery tacks. Oh, and do you have anything can mend china?"

Dolores nodded to the other women knowingly.

In the constellation of Espantosa, Helen Blas turned like a hard, disinterested star. Though the other inhabitants were aware of her, she was rarely seen; still she exerted an influence on nearly everyone. It was Helen, for instance, who funded the lion's share of the volunteer fire department. Though some were inclined to think of this as civil mindedness, the truth was she only agreed to fund the department when it was decided it would be housed in the old gas station less than a quarter mile from her house, even though this was nowhere near the geographic center of Espantosa.

Among the many things for which Helen was blamed, one item commonly assumed to have originated with her was not in fact her fault. It was assumed that it was Helen who called in the health inspector to examine Espantosa's drinking water, an investigation which cost residents dearly because the town's water had to be cut off until improvements to the system were in place. For a time, people were forced to rely on disused wells and bottled water, most of which had to be purchased either from Roy, who put in a large supply at the café, or at the Pak-N-Sip. In fact, it was not Helen who called in the health inspectors. It was Melchor Mendoza.

Within the general climate of dislike and unfriendliness with which people regarded her, Helen nonetheless did from time to time gather news from the town, and she even had an occasional visitor. Though Helen protested she found such visits highly inconvenient and distasteful, the truth was she was glad to have company, especially during the day when Roy was at work.

Among those who visited Helen from time to time was Guadalupe Lopez. It was not generally known that Helen spoke nearly perfect Spanish. She had taken classes in high school and proved to have a facility for the language. After her accident and the move to Espantosa, Helen realized that if she did not practice the language from time to time, she might lose it. So she paid Guadalupe a small sum to come and speak Spanish with her.

There was an unsettling quality to their talks, as though Guadalupe was expecting something to happen. Often she would ask probing questions which at first seemed rude to Helen. Gradually, however, she opened up to the old woman, confiding things to her she had never told anyone. At such times, the old woman would nod her head, as though these admissions merely confirmed something she already knew.

Though it was a painful trek for her, Helen and Guadalupe often conversed on the patio. This was an area so lush it rivaled Santiago's field as the greenest part of Espantosa, not surprisingly since it was Santiago who maintained it. He came twice a week to water, prune, and fuss over the plants. Helen thought this an extravagance, and told Roy as much, but in this he overruled her. Roy insisted that Helen needed fresh air, and she conceded that it was pleasant to sit outside surrounded by the cool greenery, listening to the gurgling of the fountain Roy installed for her as an anniversary present.

On the day Guadalupe drove the demons from Maria, she came to visit Helen and the two women sat together on the patio drinking lemonade in the shade of a loquat.

"I hear you drove the devil out of Maria Escalante," said Helen dryly.

Guadalupe grinned toothlessly. "If I did half the things they say I did in this town..."

"They're ignorant people," said Helen, throwing a blanket over her knees, even though it was warm outside. "But you," she added, "are a different kind of animal, I think."

"I'm just the same," said Guadalupe. She ignored Helen's use of the familiar tu, which was not fitting for addressing someone so much older. She herself always used usted when speaking to Helen.

"I disagree."

Guadalupe shrugged. "You are wiser than me, I guess. My mother used to say that cripples are wiser than other people."

Helen laughed. "You think being a cripple makes a person wise?"

"Maybe. Maybe not you. Not yet."

"Oh, I haven't been a cripple long enough, is that it?"

"Yes."

"Maybe you're right," Helen admitted. "You are the same kind of animal after all."

"Maybe you are not wise yet because you are still too mad. You are still mad that you are a cripple. One day, when you stop being mad, maybe then you will be wise."

A fly buzzed past Guadalupe's head, and the old woman reached up and snatched it from the air.

"Impressive," said Helen.

"It's a trick," said Guadalupe. She held her hand next to her ear and listened to the fly buzzing. "The fly always goes up. You just have to grab on top of it." She looked down at her hand and opened it. The fly buzzed away.

"I think your mother's saying is ridiculous. Being a cripple or having something wrong with you doesn't make you any wiser than anybody else."

"She had another saying," said Guadalupe, with a glint in her eye. "She said that a beautiful woman never has to make up her mind."

"What the hell does that mean?" said Helen in English.

"I don't know. It's just a saying."

Helen pursed her lips. "So, if I'm a cripple and ugly to boot, I should be the wisest woman on earth, is that it?" she said hotly.

"Maybe. But you're not ugly. You just have ugly ways."

Helen's hands tightened into small fists. Her face was flushed. "Then why do you come here? Is it the money?"

"No."

"Then why?"

"Because."

"That's no answer."

Guadalupe hesitated, her eyes fixed on the ground. "You are like a spider who spins her web, and you are trying to catch people. You want to devour them. That is why I come here. To play with the spider. To prove to the spider she cannot catch me, to prove to the spider she cannot devour me. Maybe one day you will know this, and then you will stop being a spider."

"Maybe you are already caught and you don't know it," said Helen, her voice shaking with anger.

Guadalupe laughed. "I would be a very bad fly if I didn't know when I was in the web." She rose to her feet. "One day, you'll stop being a spider. Then, who knows, we might even be friends. But you won't catch any flies around here, you know. Everyone knows about you. You won't catch me, and you won't catch that idiot Mayor either. Not because he's too smart. That boy is a fool. He's so dumb that he doesn't even know he's a fly! Now I need to go home. My stomach is upset and I want to go and sit on my own toilet."

Helen watched her leave, then stared down at the glass of lemonade in her hand. A fly came and landed on the rim. She regarded the fly coldly for a moment, then threw the glass to the ground and it shattered.

Chapter Fifteen

After his visit to the Aussie Goat Farm people noticed a change in Melchor. He no longer ran around the town like a gallina sin cabeza; there was a grim determination in his eyes. It showed in everything he did, even in the way he walked. On Monday morning he strode down the middle of main street, his eyes set, surveying the town. Looking out of the café window, Roy commented, "Who does that Mexican think he is, Gary Cooper?"

Melchor spent the better part of the morning going door to door, with Sandy at his side. At each stop he asked the same question: What are you going to do for the festival?

"Eat and drink, mostly," said Herbie Menchaca. He was an old man who had been a real hell-raiser in his youth and had the scars to show it.

"You still got your accordion?"

"Shit."

"You still got it though."

"Yeah. I got it. But I cain't play solo. I need a bass, and drums."

"I'll get you a bass and drums," said Melchor confidently.

The old man looked down at his gnarled hands. "I guess these fingers still remember a tune or two."

From house to house, Melchor worked his magic.

"I don't got no talent for nothing. Nothing!" said Juanita Torres. She was a middle-aged woman who had raised three sons by herself ever since her no-good husband had run off with a female trucker.

"You make the best salsa in the county," said Melchor.

"That's true," Juanita admitted with an air of pride.

"So make a big batch and sell it to the touristas."

"But how much do I charge?"

"Five dollars a jar."

"That's robbery."

"Not if the customer is willing."

By the afternoon Melchor had enlisted half the town. Sammy Cantu was going to sell roasted corn. Leticia Gonzalez was going to organize a cakewalk in the old bowling alley. Herman Peltz, who visited the Kickapoo reservation several times a year to gamble, was going to construct a roulette wheel and offer everything from goat jerky to canned tomatoes as prizes.

Melchor had no trouble locating a bass player for Herbie. Tomás Cruz was an old drinking buddy of Herbie's and he owned a bass that, though dusty, was in playable condition. The drums proved to be more difficult, until he visited Gloria Jenkins. He spied a snare drum behind the sofa and asked who played.

"Oh, those are Jesse's," she replied. Jesse was her twelve year old son. A few minutes later, Jesse gave a demonstration. He played "Wipe Out" and was recruited on the spot.

"But that's the only thing I can play," he protested.

"That's okay, just fake it," Melchor assured him. "That's what real musicians do."

The cafeteria at Sam Houston High had seen better days. The tables were stained and chipped. Most of the chairs wobbled. The floor tiles had been randomly replaced. The walls, once bright gold, had faded to puke yellow. Following a heavy rain two years ago, the entire cafeteria sank seven inches, opening a large fissure on the wall, which one of the teachers referred to as "the crack of doom." The crack had been repaired with plaster and looked like a scar that refused to heal. Above this, a banner was stretched that read "Excellence Is..." The second half of the banner had fallen at the start of the term and had not been replaced, leaving students to fill in the blanks.

It was a different story in the kitchen, where Lupe Menchaca held sway. She and the "lunch ladies" dished up some of the best meals in Espantosa. The food was so good that parents often came for lunch, ostensibly to spend some quality time with their children when what they were really after was Lupe's enchiladas, served every Wednesday. The enchiladas were so popular that extra tables had to be brought in from the library to accommodate the crowd. Indeed, Roy often complained that if the school didn't stop running an open lunch counter he was going to go into the education business and start holding classes in his storeroom. The school board ignored his complaints and raked in the dough.

Danny entered the cafeteria and waved to a couple of friends who were sitting at a far table. He picked up a warm, moist tray and took his place in line.

Mrs. Stewart, who was on duty, noticed Danny immediately. She was a large woman with enormous arms and a triple chin. As soon as she saw Danny she walked over to him.

"I hope we're not going to be treated to one of your performances," she told him.

Danny looked up and smiled. "I have to give the public what they demand," he said, waving a hand at the crowded tables.

"Not on my watch, please, Danny. Wait until Friday. I don't have duty that day."

Danny bowed gallantly. "I'll restrain myself, but they won't be happy."

Mrs. Stewart laughed. "They'll get over it. By the way, I was watching a movie the other day and I thought of you."

Danny's ears perked up. "Really? What movie?"

"*Algiers*. It's an old movie."

"I've never heard of it."

"You remind me of the main character, Pepe Le Moko. He lives in the Casbah, where he's treated like a king, but since he's a criminal, he can never leave. It's a prison, you see."

"Pepe Le Moko. Sounds like some kind of mixed up Mexican. Who plays him?"

"Charles Boyer. The point is," said Mrs. Stewart, "he's trapped into being something he doesn't want to be."

Danny grinned. "I'm not trapped."

"I think you might be, if you're not careful. So, for your own sake, try not to live up to everyone's expectations, will you? Aim a little higher." She patted Danny on the back.

"Consider it done," said Danny.

After he got his food Danny scanned the available seating. He spotted Flora immediately, of course. She was sitting with her friends. She looked up and saw Danny and gave a brief smile. Danny knew she could not risk openly acknowledging him. After the day in ISS and the visit to the football field, they had seen little of each other, and they had not managed to be alone together since he walked her home that afternoon. The time might come when they could openly admit they were an item, but neither of them was ready for that yet, so their interactions were extremely limited. Danny knew that if he let everyone know he was with Flora, he would have to suffer through the inevitable teasing, and not a little resentment from his buddies, who considered her a priss but secretly would have given their eye teeth to have a girlfriend like Flora. Flora's friends had been the butt of his jokes and suffered his verbal jabs too often to accept him as her boyfriend. The fact that he was generally considered a loser didn't help matters either. Flora, too, recognized that many of her friends had a secret affection for the bad boys in school, Danny included. Of course, the worst thing would be dealing with Tom and his set. She was worried that if Tom found out, he might try to beat up Danny. The result of all this was that they agreed to play it cool at school, at least for the time being.

Danny chose a seat at a table near the windows and exchanged insults and jokes with the boys sitting there. Lunch passed quickly, and Danny's only contact with Flora was when they both took their trays to the front. Danny put his tray on the stack and took Flora's from her and placed it on top of his. As he did so, their eyes met and Flora gave him the briefest smile.

After lunch, Danny had Media Literacy. The class had watched a video at the start of the semester that stated the aim was to make them more critical consumers of all forms of media, but all they really did in class was watch movies. Mr. Rigby always announced at the beginning of each film that there would be a quiz afterwards, but they always ran out of time. So far they had seen *West Side Story, The Bridge on the River Kwai, A Streetcar Named Desire,* and *The Good the Bad and the Ugly.* Danny had the feeling Mr. Rigby was slowly working his way through his personal video collection. It was his favorite class. The only thing he didn't like was that they had to watch everything in fifty-minute segments. Today, they were finishing up *On the Waterfront,* and Danny didn't know what film was scheduled after that. It was always a surprise.

When the movie ended, Mr. Rigby called out, "Lights!" He got to his feet and walked to the front of the class. "I need permission slips," he said. "Pass 'em forward."

Danny turned to the student next to him. "What permission slip?"

"I don't know. The movie's rated R or something. We all had to bring slips. Rigby said if you didn't he was going to send you to the library to do research."

"When did he hand them out?" asked Danny.

"Last class. Weren't you here?"

Danny, of course, had been in ISS. As it turned out, Mr. Rigby collected all the slips and never even glanced at them. He popped in the next video and turned out the lights.

Danny was distracted by someone throwing spit wads at the back of his head and he didn't notice the beginning of the video. When he looked up, he gasped. It was *The French Connection*.

In all the years Danny had been going to the Rialto, he had never been tempted to see any other version of the film. Now, as the movie started, he was instantly uneasy. He shifted in his seat. He felt another wad of paper strike him. He was aware that his heart rate had increased, and he gripped the edge of the desk tightly. He didn't want to see this movie, not now, after so many years of seeing *his* version of the film. He wanted to leave, and he considered telling Mr. Rigby he didn't have his permission slip, but he doubted anything would have happened. Mr. Rigby would probably tell him to be quiet and watch the movie. Besides, he didn't want to look like a complete idiot, and only a complete idiot would want to get out of watching a movie in order to do research in the library.

Around the class there were several titters when the film began. Mr. Rigby quieted the class. "Don't tell me you've ever seen this film," he announced, "because that abomination at the Rialto is *not* the movie, and none of you go there to watch it anyway."

"I can tell you why it's called *The French Connection*," said a girl in the front row, and everyone laughed.

Danny was actually beginning to sweat. He had to get out of this class, he told himself. Yet another spit wad struck him. He turned and glared at the student who had thrown it.

What happened next was well documented on the referral Mr. Rigby sent to the office after Danny had been removed from his class. First, Danny rose to his feet and kicked aside his desk, then he flew at a student at the back of the class, shouting "Stop throwing spit wads at me, you motherfucker!" The student with the spit wads, who was actually a friend of Danny's, jumped to his feet and pushed his desk between them. Danny vaulted over the desk and grabbed the student by the throat. "Get this crazy fucker off me!" the student screamed. Mr. Rigby moved quickly toward the boys, but his progress was impeded by the number of students who were crowding around the fight. He finally managed to break through the students and pull Danny off the other student, at which point Danny turned on him and screamed, "Let me go, you fucking prick!" and pushed Mr. Rigby back so hard he toppled over a desk. At this point, another teacher who had been passing in the hall entered, quickly sized up the situation, and pushed the call button. After a few moments, it was all over, and Danny was led from class by the campus cop while Mr. Russell shook his head.

"What set him off?"

"I don't know," Mr. Rigby admitted.

When Danny's mother picked him up she was furious. As they were pulling away from the school she said to him, "What the hell got into you?"

Danny looked out the window and shrugged. "I didn't like the movie," he said.

It wasn't Gorman Price's absence during the daylight hours that finally clued in his neighbors that something might be amiss, rather it was his absence at night. People living in the immediate vicinity of Gorman's house had grown so used to his nocturnal prowlings that they no longer jumped up when they heard the dogs barking in the middle of the night. If they heard a board creak on their back porch, they simply rolled over and went back to sleep. If they heard a rustling of leaves outside their window they would sometimes shout, "Goddamn it, Gorman, go peep in someone else's window. We're just sleeping!" Few people would admit that it gave them a kind of security to know that Gorman was on the prowl. But when they realized they had not been disturbed for several nights by barking dogs, creaking boards, or rustling leaves, they began to wonder what had happened to Gorman. They found it increasingly hard to sleep *without* Gorman's intrusions. When knocks on the door and telephone calls went unanswered, several neighbors got together and agreed that someone should call Leroy Polk. Bill French was appointed.

"Leroy," he said, "there's something odd going on at Gorman's place. Could you come over and have a looksee?"

"How many days since you saw him last?" he asked after French explained his concerns.

"Well, it's not how many days, if you take my meaning, but how many nights."

"Okay."

"But there's something else," said French, and what he said next sent a chill down Leroy Polk's spine. "There's a Godawful stench coming from that place."

After the night Gorman Price first discovered the source of the unbelievable stench, he had gone through several levels of psychic shock. His first reaction was natural incredulity. Gorman was a sensible man, and what he saw violated his ideas about order in the universe. When the apparition continued to manifest itself every night at the same time, Gorman had to surrender to the facts, as bizarre as they were. What he felt then was first a profound sense of wonder, then an equally profound sense of dread. This was followed by the realization that spectacular as the phenomenon was there was no way he could make any money out of it, and this produced the final reaction in Gorman. He was pissed off.

Chief among his complaints was that the apparition insisted on conversing with him while it was seated on *his* john.

"Goddamn it, don't you have anything to read in this fucking toilet?"

Gorman produced a 1964 issue of Life Magazine, with a special report on the Warren Commission.

"Not that shit!" the spirit bellowed. "I wouldn't wipe my ass with the Warren Report, and I sure as hell don't want to read it."

Gorman scrounged through the house and found a 1974 copy of *Reader's Digest*, which he passed over while holding a handkerchief doused with cologne over his nose and mouth.

"That's better. I like the jokes."

"Are you....?" Gorman began hesitantly.

"Am I what, boy?"

"Are you the President?"

"Hell, I ain't been President for a long time, boy. Don't you read the newspapers?"

"But you are L.B.J.?"

The spirit laughed. "You think Lyndon Baines Johnson is gonna travel back from the dead to sit on *your* crapper, boy?"

"No, I guess not."

"Well," the spirit admitted with a wink, "when you gotta go, you gotta go."

And so each night passed. Gorman would sit outside the door and listen to the ex-President read jokes from the *Reader's Digest* and howl with laughter. He was particularly delighted when Gorman found, after much searching, an entire box of the magazine, worn and covered with silverfish. He brushed them off as best he could and stacked them on the floor beside the toilet. And every night, Gorman hoped for something more. When he questioned the spirit about the Kennedy assassination, the former politico only smiled wryly and shook his head.

"You get nothing from me, boy. Nothing at all." Soon Gorman found himself staying up until dawn, and sleeping all day long. At times when Gorman started to nod off, the former President would groan loudly and let loose such an awful stench that Gorman sat bolt upright choking. In all their talks the only thing he had learned about the man was that he was unbelievably constipated.

Of course, he considered telling someone about the haunting, but he knew no one would believe him. And so their talks continued, and Gorman kept his vigil night after night, despite the fact that he was running out of food and was already eating dry cereal from the bottom of the box.

After several days, he heard the phone ringing every few minutes for about an hour, interrupting his sleep, then a knock on the door. He put a pillow over his head and ignored it. But when at last he heard what sounded like broken glass, he climbed wearily out of bed, tripped over a few empty cans of Chef Boyardee Ravioli, scattered a dozen or so cockroaches, and went to the front room. He looked at the window and noticed it was shattered, and a moment later he saw the beefy red face of Leroy Polk on the other side.

"Don't you think you should take him in?" said Bill French. The deputy had entered the house through the front door after breaking Gorman's window. He came out a short time later visibly shaken. He walked over to his patrol car and leaned against it, breathing heavily.

"Well?" said French. Several people had gathered across the street and now approached the sheriff.

Polk held up one hand, took several deep breaths, and wiped his eyes.

"What happened?"

"Nothing," said Polk.

"Is he okay?"

The sheriff rolled his eyes. "He's not dead, at any rate."

"But you're not just gonna leave him there, are you?"

"I can't arrest him for a bad smell, Bill. Besides, from what I saw a night in jail would be a reward compared to living in that place. That stench is punishment enough."

"What's causing it?" said Emily Santos, a small woman with eyes like a Pekingese who always wore a wool shawl even in the heat of summer. She drew her shawl closer and shivered. "What *could* cause a smell like that?"

"Ask Gorman," Polk growled. "He's the expert."

"It's gotta be a health hazard," said French. "We should do *something*."

"Call the EPA. All I know is the man's alive and he hasn't broken any laws. I'm going home."

The neighbors withdrew, grumbling and shaking their heads, unhappy at the prospect of another night's undisturbed sleeplessness.

Bill French watched the sheriff pull away and looked back at the house. "Something must have died in there," he said.

Chapter Sixteen

To Flora Escalante, the level of destruction visited upon her house by her grandmother was not easy to categorize. After searching her mind for all the images of nature's fury she'd ever seen on television and in movies, she decided that their living room looked as if it had suffered the combined fury of a hurricane, a tornado, and an earthquake. Upon reflection, however, she realized natural disasters failed as a model for the destructive force of her grandmother in one respect: nature was not selective. As Flora stepped gingerly over the wreckage, she was shocked not only by what had been marked for destruction but what had been spared. Standing alone in the corner of the living room beside broken pieces of wood and glass, which she recognized as the remains of her mother's corner table, was a framed portrait of Trini Lopez, completely unscathed. The cushions from the sofa had been shredded and the stuffing tossed across the floor like so many white bunny tails, but a decorative pillow with a picture of Peter Ustinov from Viva Max was intact. There were similar anomalies throughout the house.

"Where's abuela?" she asked her mother, who was sweeping broken pieces of crockery into a paper sack in the kitchen.

"In her room. She oughta be in the nut house. That woman is dangerous."

"Why did she do it?"

"Ask Guadalupe. That old bag came and visited and the next thing I knew your grandmother was running around like a wild animal."

Flora went to her room. She was relieved to find it was undamaged. She took off her shoes and sat down on the bed. A few moments later, she could hear the sound of her mother and father arguing in the kitchen. She decided to tune it all out, so she put on her headphones and popped a CD into her player. She was about to close her eyes, when she noticed Danny Montez at her window.

She took off her headphones. "I heard about what happened," she said.

"Yeah," said Danny. "What did you hear?"

"That you went berserk in Mr. Rigby's class and tried to kill Mark Flores."

"I didn't try to kill him," said Danny, though he was pleased with the exaggeration. "What happened to your grandma? I heard she was possessed."

"She kind of lost it. I don't know," Flora looked down at her toenails and noted she needed to paint them again. "So you're suspended?"

"Yeah. I'm grounded, too." Flora gave him a questioning glance. "My mom's at work," Danny explained. "She's never around."

Flora nodded. She had never liked Danny's mother. She noted also that the feeling seemed to be mutual.

"Listen," said Danny, as he peeled a tiny strip of paint off the window sill, "I was wondering..." He glanced up at Flora. She was gazing at him expectantly. "I mean, I know your dad would never agree..."

"Why don't you just say what you want to say?"

"It's just that I know your dad wouldn't like it."

"Wouldn't like what?"

"If you were running around with a homicidal maniac."

"I don't run around," said Flora primly. "But if you're asking me out, the answer is yes."

"Great," said Danny, and he surprised Flora by actually clapping his hands. Then he leaned forward and said quietly, "The only thing is..." he hesitated again. Flora sighed impatiently. "It's gonna get around, you know."

"Afraid you won't be cool anymore if you're seen with me?"

"No," said Danny with a straight face, as if this danger had only just occurred to him. "I think my reputation can handle it. I mean, you're not cool, but if you work on it..."

Flora leaned forward suddenly with a motion so graceful and quick that Danny actually gasped in the very instant her lips met his. His eyes closed, and when he opened them again, Flora was gazing at him triumphantly. "How's that for starters?" she asked.

Danny recovered slowly. "Well, I don't know," he said, running his fingers through his hair and giving her a sly look. "I think you might get the part. But you're gonna need a lot of rehearsals."

Flora leaned forward and kissed him again. "Is everything movies with you?" she asked. Then she whispered in his ear, "Don't you ever get tired of just watching?"

Danny nodded. Yes, come to think of it, he did.

The Windy Oaks nursing home was nestled between a defunct Western Auto and a convenience store. Across the street was a funeral home, which struck Melchor as a rather sick joke. He entered the nursing home through a double glass door. A small, round-faced woman was sitting behind a table. Though she was dressed in a business suit, Melchor noted she wore sneakers. She smiled as Melchor approached.

"I'm here to see Umberto Marconi," Melchor announced.

The woman's smile faded instantly. "Mr. Marconi is in room D fourteen," she said curtly, pointing over her shoulder to a long hallway in back of her. "Straight to the back, then left."

"Thank you," said Melchor. He walked down the hallway. It was brightly lit and smelled of urine and ammonia. As he passed open doors, he tried not to look inside, but now and again his attention was drawn by the sound of a television or radio blaring or, worse, the sound of someone moaning. The rooms were small and narrow, with one dark window at the rear and gaudy fluorescent lights. As he turned the corner he almost collided with a man with a grizzled beard pulling himself along in a wheelchair by grabbing onto a padded rail that ran the length of the hallway. The man looked up at him and smiled toothlessly. He seemed to be making painfully slow progress, and Melchor wondered how long he had been at it, and where he was going.

"Creamed peas today," said the man in the wheelchair. "But you have to get there early."

Melchor passed several doors before he found Umberto's room. The door was shut, and he paused before opening it. He had not seen the man in more than a decade, and he wondered what state he would find him in and how many body parts had been added to the old man's catalogue of losses. Bracing himself, he opened the door. His jaw dropped.

Umberto was seated with his back to the door at a large mahogany desk. In front of him was an ancient typewriter. The desk was covered with sheets of paper and books. Reams of paper were stacked on the floor. There were papers of all kinds posted on the walls. It was less like a room than a nest. When Melchor opened the door, a draft was created and every paper in the room began to flap madly. For a moment, the entire room seemed to be swirling before his eyes. In the middle of this dizzying display sat Umberto, pecking away like a bird at the typewriter.

"Umberto," said Melchor.

Umberto did not turn, but raised a hand and said, "Not now!"

"Umberto!"

"Can't you see I've got a deadline!" exclaimed Umberto, swiveling in his chair. His one eye blinked rapidly. A smile spread across his face.

"Melchor, my boy!" Umberto beamed.

"Hello, Umberto."

"What on earth made you come and visit me after all these years? Haven't been elected Governor, have you?"

"Afraid not," Melchor smiled.

"Thank heavens," Umberto muttered.

"What are you doing?" asked Melchor, pointing to the typewriter.

"Oh, that. You are looking at the editor and publisher of *The Windy Oaks Daily Gazette*."

"Not hourly?" Melchor laughed softly.

"It should be," said the old man, "it should be. God knows there's enough news to print. Melchor, it's astonishing. There's something happening all the time in this place. These people are interesting, not like that lot in Espantosa. There's so much stuff, I can't keep up with it all." He reached into a drawer and pulled out a thick stack of papers. He handed them to Melchor. "That's just this year, my boy, just this year."

Melchor leafed through the papers. They were really nothing more than a few typewritten sheets that had been copied and stapled together. There were no photographs, but several crude drawings accompanied some of the stories. Melchor guessed these were drawn by Umberto himself. The headlines and the staff were hand-lettered. Umberto tapped his finger on one issue and said, "That one caused quite a ruckus around here, I can tell you." The headline read: Prescription Scam Exposed.

"Of course," he added, "what I really need is a press, but I make do."

There was a knock at the door and both men turned.

"Ah, Dr. Quackenbush," said Umberto. "I want you to meet a friend of mine. This is Melchor Mendoza, the Mayor of Espantosa."

The doctor was a tall man with deep blue eyes and dark hair beginning to gray. He smiled at Umberto's introduction and extended his hand to Melchor. "Dr. Murray," he said. "Pleased to meet you."

"Dr. Murray?" said Melchor, taking the doctor's hand and shaking it. It was firm and damp.

"Dr. Quackenbush," Umberto corrected him. "The finest horse doctor in three counties."

Dr. Murray smiled indulgently. "So," he said, turning to Umberto, "when can we expect the next issue?"

"The doctor is one of my most avid readers," Umberto explained with a wink.

"He keeps us on our toes," said Dr. Murray. "I've never heard of Espantosa."

"No reason you should have," said Umberto. "Espantosa is like most of the inhabitants in this establishment. Whatever good days it had are behind it, but it doesn't have sense enough to crawl away and die."

Dr. Murray raised an eyebrow.

"Note," said Umberto pointedly, "I said *most*. Now, why don't you give his honor a tour of the place while I finish up here?" He turned to Melchor. "We'll have lunch together, how's that?"

Melchor assented, though the last thing he wanted was a tour of Windy Oaks. He and the doctor stepped outside and immediately they heard the sound of Umberto pounding away at the enormous typewriter, punctuated with curses.

"I doubt you're really interested in a tour," said Dr. Murray as he led Melchor down the hall. "Still, I'm glad to be able to visit with you for a while. I've never met any of Umberto's friends. How long have you known him?"

The two men chatted as they walked to Dr. Murray's office, which was a large, comfortable room with a view of the convenience store parking lot.

"I can't get over how well he looks," said Melchor. "To be honest, I didn't know what to expect. I thought he might be in an iron lung by now."

"Yes," Dr. Murray agreed. "He's doing remarkably well for a man of his age. His infirmities don't seem to faze him at all. If anything, they seem to make him more energetic. He told me once he's determined to outlive himself."

Melchor laughed. "That sounds like Umberto!"

"It was a different story when he first came here. I fully expected him to kick the bucket any time. But he held on. Still, there's a difference between surviving and living."

"But he seems to be getting on well."

"Oh yes-- *now*."

"What happened?"

The doctor opened a drawer and took out a stack of papers. He passed them to Melchor and leaned back in his chair, an expression of pained fatigue on his face. "I knew Umberto had been a newspaperman, and when I suggested..." The doctor paused. "It seemed like a reasonable course of treatment. Many of our residents feel detached from life. Anything that makes them feel useful... But I never dreamed.... My God, you should read some of this stuff! Last month, he wrote an article about the use of restraints.

173

Had half the residents in an uproar. Made it sound like we were running a dungeon in the dark ages. Look at this one." He pointed to a headline that read: "Viagra Denial is Loss of Manhood." "He actually advocates selling Viagra through vending machines at a dollar a pop. The last thing we need is a bunch of old men wandering the halls with stiff peckers looking for some action."

Melchor tried hard to suppress a smile.

"He may have lost a number of body parts over the years, but one thing I can assure he still retains is balls."

Melchor considered this for a moment as the doctor looked out the window. Melchor noted his fingernails were chewed to the bone. "Couldn't he just leave? I mean, he looks okay. Couldn't he function on the outside?"

"I've suggested it. More than once. He refuses. My hands are tied."

Melchor nodded. "I see."

"The worst part of it is, he's on a campaign to have me replaced. Says I take kickbacks from the pharmaceutical companies." The doctor began to chew one of his fingernails. "At first, I discounted it, but now there's going to be an inquiry. I swear to God, that old man may not outlive himself, but he's sure as hell going to outlive me!"

"So, did Dr. Quackenbush tell you he was about to lose his job?"

The two men were seated in the dining hall. Umberto spoke to one of the servers briefly and arranged for Melchor to be brought a plate. As they waited to be served, Melchor tried to avoid looking at the other diners. Many were seated in wheel chairs, leaning listlessly to one side and staring at the floor or the ceiling. A few, having been served already, were eating their food with painful deliberation. Melchor stared at the table cloth and wondered how Umberto managed to stay so cheerful living in such a place.

"I expect he told you it was on account of me."

"What? Oh, yes. He mentioned it."

"That man's in the pocket of the pharmaceuticals. It's too bad, really, because he's not a bad Joe." Melchor was about to ask Umberto why he was going after the doctor if he liked him so much, but at that moment their food arrived. "Only good thing about this place," said Umberto, tucking his napkin under his chin. "But tell me about yourself, and what's going on in Espantosa.

"There's going to be a festival," said Melchor. He tasted the cream peas and looked at Umberto in astonishment. "These peas..."

"Remarkable, isn't it? But the food here wasn't always so good. It was my first campaign, and one of my few successes."

"Campaign," said Melchor with a grin. "You sound like a politician."

Umberto sat up straight and pulled his napkin from under his chin. "If you're going to get insulting, I'll have to ask you to leave," he said with mock seriousness. "Anyway, what about this festival?"

"It's a long story," Melchor began. He recounted the arrival of Miss Coakely and the effect on the town. Umberto seemed especially delighted by the stories the townspeople were inventing to try and get into the Book.

"I never knew they had it in them," he said, laughing and wiping a tear from his eye. "So tell me," he was getting the better of his mirth, "whatever happened to all your big plans?"

Melchor spread his hands across the table and took a deep breath.

"No, don't answer that. It's not a fair question. Your problem is, you've never really known what it is you wanted. You didn't really want to be a newspaperman. You just wanted to win friends and influence people. I suppose that's why you wanted to be Mayor." He pushed away his plate and leaned back in his chair. "You know what you really wanted, my boy?"

"I'm sure you're going to tell me," said Melchor with a smile.

"Love," said Umberto, looking at him seriously. "That's all anyone ever really wants. The trouble is, we don't know how to get it. Look around you. How long do you think it's been since any of them last felt a warm embrace? Years? Decades for some. And I'll tell you right now, every last one of them, all they want in life is to crawl back into their mama's arms."

"You know," said Melchor after a moment's silence, "I think I half convinced myself I came here to make sure you were okay. Now, I wonder if I didn't come here for another reason entirely."

"I'm fine, my boy," said Umberto. "I'll probably go blind soon, and I'm sure to lose my few remaining teeth, and I doubt I could get credit from a tailor, but on the other hand I'm not ready to crawl into a pine box yet."

"I don't think they use pine boxes anymore, Umberto."

"You're probably right." Umberto took a gulp of coffee. "You were right, my boy, all those years ago."

"About what?"

"Fighting the good fight. I had given up, that was the truth. I had joined the ranks of the Indifferents. I tell you, when I came here, I was ready to give up the ghost. Then an odd thing happened. I lost my eye. I became a cyclops.

"Losing an eye is different, you know, from losing a tooth, or even a kidney. I used to tell people before they bury me, they'll have to reassemble me." Umberto laughed. "I knew what my body was up to. I considered it a form of protest for leading a dissolute life. But this, this was different. This was an act of outright rebellion!

"I can't fully explain this, but for some reason I felt it was a moral issue. Maybe it was my Catholic upbringing. You understand, I felt I had to do *something*."

"So you started *The Windy Oaks Daily Gazette*," said Melchor.

"Dr. Quackenbush suggested it. Poor man. I do feel sorry for him. I think he might have to give up his vacation in Aspen this Christmas."

When Melchor returned to the Rialto, he found Danny Montez sitting on the pavement out front.

He greeted the boy and opened the front door. Danny hesitated. He gave the boy a quizzical look.

"You think we could go for a drive?" Danny asked.

"I just got home," said Melchor tiredly.

"I really need to talk."

Melchor noted the urgency in his voice. Though he resisted the impulse to parent the boy, he knew Danny had few people he could talk to.

"Okay," he said resignedly. "Just let me fix myself something to eat first."

He went upstairs and made a sandwich. He offered Danny one but the boy shook his head. When he was done eating he asked Danny where he wanted to go.

"I was thinking we could drive out to the lake," Danny said.

"Okay. But it'll be dark by the time we get there."

Danny shrugged.

"Don't blame me if you get the willies."

Melchor stopped and picked up Sandy at Connie's. By the time they got to the lake, it was dusk. The sun was setting behind a bank of dark clouds and the water reflected the deep reds and indigos of the sky. Melchor parked near the dam and the two of them got out. Sandy walked up to the edge of the lake and sniffed the water cautiously.

Lake Espantosa was more like a wide ditch, a deep gash carved into the terrain, and its waters were famously treacherous. The concrete dam spanned no more than fifty feet and had been poured so badly that several moss-covered outcroppings protruded from the brackish water. Even in summer, the lake was often covered in morning mists. Now, as the sun sank deeper, the waters darkened and the surrounding brush receded into deep shadow.

Melchor had never liked the lake. He would not have admitted it, but like most of the locals he believed the legends surrounding it, tales told in whispers by children in darkened bedrooms or by old people on back porches when the sun had set and the only sounds were the creaking of rocking chairs or the hoot of an owl. He sat down uneasily on the sandy ground and waited for Danny to open up.

"I got suspended today."

"What for?"

"I don't know."

Melchor waited.

"Mr. Rigby was showing a movie."

"Uh huh."

"I don't know. I guess it just upset me."

"What movie?"

"*The French Connection,*" Danny mumbled.

Melchor felt his stomach tighten slightly. "So?"

"I didn't want to see it."

"Why not? It's your favorite, isn't it?"

"I just didn't want to see it, that's all."

Melchor nodded. "It's a good movie."

"It's a great movie," Danny corrected him. "The best ever!"

"Then what's the problem?"

Danny got up and began to pace. He picked up a stick and tossed it into the water. "I always liked your movie. I mean, I always thought that

179

was what life was really like. You know, everything all sort of fucked up and all. It made sense."

"And now?"

"Shit, I don't know," Danny said quietly.

"Listen," Melchor said softly, "the movie you see at the Rialto, it's not the real movie."

"I know." Danny sat down again. He stared into the dark water for a long time.

"That's not what life is like," said Melchor.

"I know, but it's easier, isn't it, if you think that way?"

"Because then you don't have to try?"

"I guess so."

The stars were coming out above. The moon was brightening over the horizon. "It's really nice out here, isn't it?"

Melchor laughed. "If you don't mind being carried off by a giant owl!"

"Aw, that's all bullshit, man."

"What about the alligators?"

"Same substance."

Melchor reflected sadly that Danny's attitude was not unique among the young people in Espantosa. The old stories had lost their potency. It seemed a shame to him.

"So what brought about this new attitude toward life?" he asked.

Danny grinned. "I guess I'm in love."

"Who's the girl?"

"Flora Escalante."

Melchor gave a low whistle that floated out over the water. Somewhere in the distance, seemingly in response, an owl hooted and both men broke into laughter. Sandy too had heard the call, and rose to his feet. He gave a noncommittal bark and settled down uneasily beside Melchor once again, his ears cocked.

After a moment, Danny said, "You know, I wanted to make a movie about the festival."

"That would have been..." Melchor searched for the right word, "interesting."

"I used to think I could only be happy in the movies," Danny said.

Melchor pondered the double meaning of this statement. "I know how you feel."

"I'm not so sure now." Danny suddenly took off his hat and flung it out over the lake. It sailed gracefully over the water and landed softly. It floated for a moment on the surface, then slowly sank.

"Let's head back," said Danny, helping Melchor to his feet.

As they drove away from the lake neither of them noticed the shadow of enormous wings that passed swiftly over the roof of the car.

Chapter Seventeen

If the Santiago Morales Memorial Field was a gem to behold, it did have a flaw. Over the years the visitors' bleachers had fallen into an awful state of disrepair. The wooden planks were worn and sagging in the middle; some had warped in the West Texas sun. The paint was cracked and peeling. It was an eyesore and it stuck in Santiago's craw that the school board would not allow him to fix it. "Who cares if those bleachers are falling apart," was the general attitude. "That's where the other guys sit!" Santiago pointed out that the visitors' bleachers were usually more occupied than the home side. The school board would not budge. Santiago's heart sank every time he looked at them.

Now, as football season approached, Santiago racked his brain for some way to remedy the situation. What he really needed was lumber. He knew where he could lay his hands on all he needed. There was a large supply of lumber sitting in the bus garage, but it was earmarked for other purposes. He doubted anyone would miss it right away, but eventually it would be needed. So he prepared to go to work that morning resigned to another football season with the bleachers staring at him accusingly.

He cooked his eggs, filled his thermos, and opened the front door of his shack.

Santiago was not a religious man. He believed in God, but he thought it was foolish to assume a Divine Being would be interested in the day-to-day lives of human beings. He never prayed. He was hard-pressed, therefore, to explain what he saw when he opened the front door of his shack. He stared for a moment, open-mouthed, then made the sign of the cross and slowly raised his eyes to Heaven.

"You just left the wood in front of his shack?"

"He was asleep." Melchor was cooking breakfast when Connie arrived. He tossed two more eggs into the pan.

"What time did you do all this?"

"Four-thirty." Melchor grinned sheepishly.

"I think you just didn't want to face him."

"I thought it was a diplomatic way of reminding him," said Melchor. He served the eggs and sat down at the table across from Connie. They ate together and Melchor reflected that this was one more way in which their lives had become intertwined: they now shared almost all their meals.

"I hope you left a note," said Connie, taking a bite of her eggs.

"What?"

"I said, I hope you left a note. Leaving the lumber is one thing, but what if he decides to use it to patch up that shack he lives in?"

Melchor considered the idea for a moment. It had never occurred to him that Santiago might have other uses for a pile of lumber. "He has to know what it's for," he said, trying to sound convincing. "How else would it have got there?"

"Maybe it fell from the sky. How should I know? Maybe it was a miracle."

"No, no," said Melchor, waving his hand as though he were shooing away a mosquito. "He'll know what it's for."

Santiago enlisted four members of the football team and by ten o'clock he succeeded in moving all the lumber to the visitors' bleachers. He then set about removing the bad wood, which took the better part of the morning.

As he worked, he could not stop thinking about the miracle of the lumber. "Wood just doesn't fall from the sky," he said out loud. And then, as if holding a debate with himself, he answered, "No, it doesn't." He looked up at the sky as if to confirm his hypothesis. "No," he repeated conclusively, "wood does not fall from the sky." Satisfied that his logic was sound, he continued in a different vein. "You've been a real son-of-a-bitch, you know. So, you expect me to be grateful to you now? Is that how it works?" He paused and stared once more at the heavens. "Okay, so I'm grateful. But," he raised a finger in warning, "don't think this makes us even."

By one o'clock, he had measured and cut the lumber and was ready to start hammering it in place. He was hungry now, and decided to go back to his shack for lunch.

As soon as he approached the shack, he knew he should have kept working. Sitting on his front porch was Melchor Mendoza.

"Hello!" said Melchor, getting to his feet.

Briefly, Santiago considered telling Melchor about the miracle of the lumber, but then he thought better of it. Instead, he grunted hello and waited to see what the damn fool wanted.

"Did you get the lumber?" said Melchor.

Santiago gave him a wary look. "How did you know about that?" he asked suspiciously.

"I left it here this morning, when you were asleep."

Santiago stared at Melchor open-mouthed. Then he threw back his head and laughed.

"It's for the stage," Melchor explained.

Santiago laughed so hard he began to cough. When he had recovered, he wiped his eyes and said, "Yes, I got it. The lumber for the stage."

"Great," said Melchor. "Then you can start on it right away?"

"Of course. In fact, I already have." Santiago chuckled. "The platform stage."

"Right. So, I can count on you." Melchor looked dubious.

"Of course." Then he added, "Where do you want it?"

"In the parking lot of the bowling alley."

"Then why did you bring it here?" asked Santiago

"I just thought it might be handier."

Santiago considered this a stupid reason. If he had used the lumber for the stage, he would only have had to cart it all the way back to the location where it was wanted, which was right next door to the hardware store where the wood had been to begin with. "I'll get it there," he said. Under his breath, he muttered, "You stupid pendejo."

Either Melchor heard this or the same thought had suddenly entered his mind. "I guess it would have been better to have left it at Mrs. Nelson's," he said weakly. He looked around. "By the way, where is..."

"No, it's okay," Santiago interrupted hastily. "I'll get it down there."

"I'm sorry. I think I made more work for you."

"No, no. It's okay. But now I have to go. I need to eat my lunch and get back to work."

"That's fine then. Very good." Melchor shook hands with Santiago and left, feeling slightly baffled by the old man's behavior, but reassured at least that the lumber was being used for the purpose it was intended.

Santiago watched him leave, then raised his eyes to heaven. "You almost had me," he said, wagging a finger. "You almost had me."

Since the disastrous meeting with Melchor Mendoza, Miss Coakely had noticed a change in attitudes toward her in general. The well of free goods and services had begun to dry up. People were getting used to her. When she pulled into Bill French's garage, he merely looked over at her and waved. He made no attempt to fill her tank, and Miss Coakely was forced to pump the gas herself.

"Afternoon," said French when she had finished. "That'll be, um," he glanced at his register, "Five dollars."

Miss Coakely, her hopes of free gas dashed, had put in as much fuel as she could afford.

"Not planning on traveling too far, I hope," French added, with amusement.

"I just like to keep the tank topped off," Miss Coakely stated.

"That's a good practice there. Keeps the sediments from clogging up the motor."

Miss Coakely took out the Book. "Just how long did you say Steve McQueen spent in town?"

"Oh, that." French grinned sheepishly. "I was just pulling your leg, Miss."

She glared at him. "You lied?"

French cleared his throat. "Well, not so much lied as stretched the truth."

"Was he here or not?"

"Sure, sure. I filled his tank myself."

"And he was arrested?"

"Now that I'm not so sure about." French slipped his finger inside his collar. "It's what I heard, but you oughta ask Leroy Polk. His daddy was sheriff back then."

Miss Coakely huffed loudly. She closed the Book and turned on her heel.

Driving away from the station, Miss Coakely felt greatly unnerved. Of course, she had never believed the whole McQueen saga, but what unsettled her is that French was so willing to expose the truth.

In the café that afternoon, she was relieved not to find Connie waiting tables. She noticed several hostile stares aimed in her direction. Fent Hurley looked up from his table and belched loudly, which sent the entire establishment into snickers. As she slid into a booth, Miss Coakely could not help but feel some of the laughter was directed at her.

"What'll it be?" asked Roy from behind the counter.

Miss Coakely asked for a menu.

"Oh, hell," said Roy. "Lissen, my waitress is on vacation, so if you could just tell me what you want it would save me having to come all the way over there."

Miss Coakely sized up the situation quickly. "I was thinking I'd try the Lovers' Special finally."

"It's off the menu."

"Well, if I'm going to write about it in the Book, I should at least..."

"Like I said, it's off the menu."

All eyes were on her now. She shifted uncomfortably in her seat. "I'd just like a cup of coffee." Then, half-heartedly, she added, "It's a shame that I won't be able to put it in the Book, is all."

"That's okay," Hurley smirked. "Roy's already famous for his chili."

Roy ignored the laughter. He came around the counter and sloshed coffee into a half-clean cup, set it onto a saucer and placed a single lukewarm cream beside it. "Here ya go," he muttered, leaving the cup on the counter.

Miss Coakely drank her coffee in silence.

Perhaps the only person in town who still seemed interested in the Book was Melchor Mendoza. On two occasions she ran into him and each time he assured her he was working on a solution to "our little problem." Both times, however, that waitress had been with him. Miss Coakely did not pursue the matter any further. Finally, near the end of the day, she spotted him in the Soft Soap. Connie was nowhere to be seen.

When she opened the door, Melchor had his head inside one of the washers. She sat down on a faded vinyl chair and waited.

"Oh, I didn't see you come in," said Melchor. He held a damp pair of yellowed underwear in his hand. He looked down at it and grinned. "It was stuck in the well," he said. "I could open a used clothing store with all the stuff people leave behind." Then he laughed. "Not that anyone would want to buy this, of course." He chucked the briefs into the wastebasket.

"I wanted to talk about the money," said Miss Coakely. It was not the right approach, but the day's events had left her feeling panicked.

"Ah," Melchor replied. "The thing is, our budget is pretty tight." He picked up a small canvas bag and began emptying the quarters from the machines.

"You were the one who brought it up in the first place."

"I realize that."

"I never asked."

"I know you didn't." He went to the next machine, inspected it, and removed the change. "I don't suppose you'd be willing to take quarters," he said with a laugh.

Miss Coakely's back stiffened. "I'm not sure about that waitress."

"Connie?" Melchor leaned back on the washer. "What do you mean?"

"What you're proposing is, as I said, highly unethical. It requires discretion."

"Oh, she wouldn't say anything. Besides," he gave her a sly look, "no one knows who to tell. You never mentioned who you work for, remember?"

"Just so we're clear," Miss Coakely said primly.

"Uh huh." Melchor began emptying the driers. "I guess we better talk about how much."

"A week's salary."

"And how much is that?"

Miss Coakely paused, weighing her answer carefully. Melchor turned and looked at her. "Two hundred and fifty dollars."

"I see."

"That does not include expenses," she added.

"Of course not." Melchor finished emptying the machines and weighed the bag in his hand. "Not a bad haul," he said. Then, sitting down opposite her, "But there's one other matter."

Miss Coakely tensed. "What's that?"

"Just what do you intend to say?"

"I can hardly tell you that. It depends on what the festival looks like."

Melchor considered this. He stared at the floor for an uncomfortably long time. "I understand that, but..." he did not finish his thought.

Miss Coakely was sensitive to a subtle shift in the Mayor. "I'm sure it would be something positive."

Melchor stood up and took a deep breath. "Now how can you say that?"

"I'm not allowed to say negative things."

Melchor began to pace the floor. Miss Coakely leaned forward in her seat. She felt her stomach tightening.

"I know this sounds stupid," Melchor announced at last, "but I think maybe we'll just have to take our chances. The festival is only two days away. If you really think you have to go, then I guess we shouldn't try to make you stay. Like you said, it's not really ethical."

Miss Coakely got quickly to her feet.

"I hope there's no hard feelings," he said, extending his hand.

She glared at his hand, but not did not accept it. Turning on her heel, she left without saying another word.

What Roy Blas lacked in culinary skill he made up for in efficiency. He prided himself not on the meals he served but on the speed at which he dished them up. He considered himself a short order cook par excellence, with an emphasis on short. Though it was true that from time to time he did make attempts to vary the fare, for the most part he stuck to what he knew. Now, with the festival just days away, Roy realized that he knew nothing about cooking prairie oysters. So it was that Melchor and Connie found themselves sitting at the counter in the café as Roy dished up several variations. Neither was happy about being a guinea pig, but Roy insisted that they come. Fearing another run-in with Helen, they reluctantly agreed. Since it was after hours, Roy let Melchor bring Sandy inside the restaurant. The dog curled up under the counter and went to sleep.

"I've tried several approaches," Roy explained, laying a plate on the counter in front of them, "but there's only so much you can do with testicles."

Melchor nodded and Connie stifled a laugh.

The oysters resembled large egg yolks, except that they were gray in color and appeared to have been battered.

"How did you cook these?" Melchor asked.

"I think it's best not to go into that right now," said Roy.

"Uh, can I have a fork?" said Melchor, stalling.

"It's basically finger food."

Melchor picked up one of the oysters. It was rubbery to the touch and the batter slid off his fingers. He sniffed it dubiously. "Could we take a look at the others?"

"I think we should take them in order."

Melchor gave Connie a helpless look, and took a small bite of the oyster. It shot out of his hand and landed on the counter where it quivered sickeningly. He reached for a napkin and spit into it. "I think we better move on to number two," he said.

"Okay," Roy agreed grudgingly. "I didn't think you'd like that one anyway."

"Then why did you make me try it?" asked Melchor.

"A good cook has to take risks," said Roy. He produced another plate and laid it on the counter.

"Your turn," Melchor told Connie.

"No way!" Connie protested. "You didn't try that one!"

"I put it in my mouth."

"I don't think it counts unless you actually swallow," said Connie.

"I've heard that before," laughed Roy.

Connie looked down at the plate. These oysters had apparently been deep-fried and whatever lay beneath the batter at least looked edible. She thought it better to try this one. There was no telling what the next ones might look like. She picked up the oyster and sniffed it. It didn't *smell* bad, she thought. She took a small bite and began to chew slowly. An instant later she reached for a napkin and, following Melchor's example, spit the oyster into it. "Water," she gasped, covering her mouth with her hands.

Roy quickly poured a glass of water and handed it to Connie. She gulped down several mouthfuls and said, "What did you put in that?"

"Okay, okay," Roy said, ignoring her question, "we'll consider that a no. Let's move on."

"Just how many different ways did you try to cook these?" asked Melchor.

Roy shrugged. "I lost count, but we're not going to try them all!"

"Well, thank God for that!" said Connie.

Roy looked hurt as he laid the next plate on the counter.

"Your turn," said Connie.

"You didn't swallow!" Melchor protested. Connie glared at him. "All right, all right," he said. He picked up the oyster which, like the last one, appeared to have been battered and deep fried. "This is not the same..." he began.

"No, no," Roy stated. "This is different."

Melchor took a cautious bite of the oyster and began to chew, bracing himself. Surprisingly, it tasted fine. "Hey!" he exclaimed, "this one's not too bad. Not too bad at all."

"You're eating the batter," Roy said.

"Oh." Melchor took a larger bite. He chewed for a moment and gagged, spitting the oyster across the counter and onto the floor of the kitchen. He snatched Connie's glass from the counter and drank the remainder of the water in one large gulp. "I feel like I just licked the bottom of Gorman's work boots," he gasped.

Sandy trotted over to the morsel and sniffed it delicately. He emitted a small yelp and slinked away.

Unfazed, Roy placed another plate on the counter. "These are different."

"Oh, good," said Melchor weakly.

"I marinated them," Roy explained.

"Roy," said Melchor, "correct me if I'm wrong, but isn't the whole idea to serve a whole lot of these things fast?"

"I guess so."

"Then why don't you just drop them in some fried chicken batter and deep fry them?"

"Anyone can do that," said Roy sullenly.

"Have you actually tried any of these concoctions?" asked Connie.

"I'm too close to it. Let's move on."

For the next thirty minutes, Connie and Melchor suffered through several variations, the worst of which featured two rosy testicles in a vinaigrette sauce. Melchor refused to try this. Connie had slid into a booth and lay with her eyes closed, holding her stomach and moaning. In the end, Roy was forced to sample the dish himself. He took one bite, then covered his mouth and rushed to the sink. After rinsing his mouth several times, he was forced to admit defeat.

"I've come to the conclusion," he said tiredly, "that there's only so much you can do with testicles."

Melchor walked Connie home. She was a little unsteady on her feet, and twice they paused when she thought she was going to be sick. "My God," she gasped, "he's going to kill us all."

"It's okay," Melchor told her, holding her shoulders as she bent forward. "He just wanted to try some different approaches. It'll be fine."

"I think he poisoned me."

When they reached the front steps of Connie's house, Connie opened the door and rushed in, her hand covering her mouth. Melchor stepped inside and waited. He could hear the sound of her heaving through the bathroom door. Sandy looked up at him curiously. He almost appeared concerned.

"I feel better," said Connie, emerging a few minutes later. "I got rid of whatever I managed to swallow by mistake, and I brushed my teeth and gargled. I think I finally got the taste out of my mouth."

"You want us to stay a while?" Melchor asked. Sandy wagged his tail.

"No. Thanks," said Connie with a weak smile. "I think I need to get to bed."

Reluctantly, Melchor said goodnight. "You're sure there's nothing you need?" he asked as he stood in the doorway.

"Just some sleep. I'll see you tomorrow, Melchor."

Melchor nodded, thinking how utterly beautiful Connie looked as she stood in the doorway, her hair a little tousled, her face flushed. He was pleased when a moment later he turned to see that she was still watching from the doorway. She waved her arm and Melchor felt an overwhelming desire to rush back to her and kiss her on the mouth. He hesitated, then looked down at Sandy, who was staring at him with a look of expectancy.

"I know, boy, I know," said Melchor, patting Sandy on the head. He waved at Connie and headed toward home. Sandy trotted along beside him.

It was one of those nights when Melchor felt it was easy to like living in Espantosa. The stars were brilliant in the velvety sky, and the moon was a silver shard rising over the top of the Rialto. There was a slight crispness in the air that hinted at an early fall. It was the sort of weather that made Melchor think of football games and tangerines trucked in fresh from the Valley. He reflected that winter was not going to be long in coming. Days always seemed to rush by once they went off Daylight Savings Time. Soon enough it would be Christmas, and for the first time in a long time he dared to hope he would not be spending the season alone.

Then, as they passed the old bowling alley, his mood changed radically. Melchor noted with dismay that the lumber was nowhere to be seen. Cursing under his breath, he made a vow to see Santiago first thing in the morning and settle the matter once and for all. Not for the first time in the past couple of days, he thought what a relief it would be to put the festival behind him. The only problem was, what would he do then? And what excuse would he have to spend so much time with Connie?

As he approached the Rialto, he turned suddenly, like a man who senses he is being followed and wants to spot his pursuer. But Melchor was not being followed.

Over the past few days, he had grown so accustomed to the sound of Sandy's claws tapping rhythmically beside him that he no longer noticed it, until it stopped. He looked down the street. It was alarmingly empty.

Sandy was gone.

Chapter Eighteen

At forty-two, Maria Walsh was still an attractive woman. If she had lost her youthful blush in the years since Tom's death, she had gained a definite air of self-confidence which some saw as haughtiness. Walking down the street at night, no one would have mistaken her for an angel, as Tom had done so many years before. She had the allure of a movie star who was accustomed to adulation and who was bored by it.

Men in Espantosa knew she was out of their league, but that did not stop them from making the attempt. The rumors about her fortune (which was greatly exaggerated) encouraged even the most hopeless suitors. She coolly rebuffed them all. Women in Espantosa almost universally despised her. None could compete with her, and they resented that the small pool of available men was comprised solely of those she had, at one time or another, spurned.

Maria took no lovers. She had few friends. In all, she seemed destined to become that figure so common in small towns everywhere– the rich, reclusive widow. She might have been a character from a novel by Hardy. The only ingredient she lacked was piety. To the people of Espantosa, her existence seemed inexplicably austere. If she felt that life had treated her unfairly, she never surrendered to self-pity. She was, if not exactly happy, content with her solitary life.

All of that changed with the arrival of Sandy Foster.

The Aussie was as hot as she was cool, as unabashedly open as she was reserved, as dynamic and driven as she was detached. The citizens of Espantosa took to him from the start. He was as immediately popular as Maria was unpopular.

The first time she saw him, Maria thought he looked like Alec Guinness in The Bridge on the River Kwai. He wore khaki shorts and a shirt unbuttoned at the collar, and when he walked he swung his arms so that he always appeared to be marching. Maria could almost hear "Colonel Bogey's March" whistling in her ears every time she saw him. But Sandy had not come to Espantosa to build a bridge. As he announced shortly after his arrival, he had come to build an empire.

An empire founded on goats.

Sandy noticed Maria almost immediately, and he was impressed. He knew instinctively that Maria was not the sort of woman with whom he could have a lighthearted fling. Even before he heard her story, he guessed that some grave matter lay in her past.

Unlike so many other men, Sandy made no attempt to court Maria. If anything, he went out of his way to avoid her. It was inevitable, however, that they should meet often in a town as small as Espantosa. If Maria was surprised by his lack of interest, she felt sure she understood its source. She waited for the smallest sign that would confirm her hypothesis, but it never came.

Sandy's plans began to take shape, and construction started on the complex of buildings and pens outside town. Sandy was careful to purchase as many goods as he could from local merchants, and he hired locally, too. He paid handsomely, and soon laborers began to arrive from other quarters. Within three months of his arrival, the first goats appeared, and shortly thereafter the farm went into production. The first cartons of Aussie Goat Milk hit the shelves of Espantosa on a cold day in November, and the entire town turned out to sample the goods.

Maria followed these developments with growing interest. The Aussie still kept his distance from her. But when he organized a soiree to celebrate the farm going into production, he made sure Maria was on the guest list.

Sandy had hired a troupe of musicians. They set up in the corner of the VFW and played "Waltzing Matilda" so many times Sandy finally had to tell them to stop. Behind the band, across one wall, hung a banner that featured the smiling goat that would haunt the nightmares of Espantosa's children long after the Goat Farm disappeared.

Maria did not arrive until late in the evening. Though they were separated by a roomful of people, Sandy felt her presence the moment she entered. He had doffed his usual khakis in favor of a coat and tie. When he approached Maria she almost didn't recognize him.

"I'm glad you could make it, Mrs. Walsh," he said, grinning bashfully.

"You look like a different man," Maria said, and it was true.

"Nah, still the same. Just a little window dressing." Then he added, "Would you like something to drink?"

"Not goat milk."

"No," Sandy laughed. "I was thinking of champagne."

Maria agreed and followed him to the table. He poured two glasses and handed one to her. Maria watched him closely, and it struck her that he was not unaccustomed to pouring champagne, which he did with ease and flair.

"To your empire," said Maria, raising her glass.

"Thanks." Again the bashful grin.

"Are you trying to be charming?" asked Maria. She gave him a frank, questioning look.

Sandy leaned forward and whispered close to her ear. "It's just an act. My ancestors never came down from the trees."

"I didn't think there were trees in Australia."

"One or two. Mostly crocs and rocks."

"Espantosa must seem like paradise then."

Sandy regarded her seriously. "It's starting to," he said.

For the next few weeks, the Goat Farm occupied all of Sandy's time. He saw little of Maria, and it was not until he decided to take an evening off and attend a showing at the Rialto that he had the opportunity to speak to her at any length.

When he arrived at the theater, Maria was nowhere to be seen. The ticket booth was empty and Sandy slid the price of admittance through the window and went inside.

In his entire life, Sandy had been to the movies only twice before. It was a form of entertainment he just didn't get. On the other hand, there was not much else to do in Espantosa.

Having so little experience with movies, Sandy found it hard to follow what was happening. The movie seemed to be about a gangster and his girlfriend. But it was also about a little boy and girl. It was a long time before he figured out the boy and girl were the gangsters when they were kids. He found much of the movie amusing, even though he didn't think it was supposed to be funny. He wondered if the audience really believed you could hit anything at those distances by firing from your hip.

He left the theater scratching his head, and ran into Maria. She asked him what he thought of the movie.

"Well," he said thoughtfully, "it seemed a little dodgy. Was this a good movie?"

"It's supposed to be," said Maria, smiling.

"I can't say I thought much of it, and no offense, I hope. Did you know the boy and girl and the gangster and his girlfriend were the same people?"

"Yes, I knew that," she laughed.

Sandy scratched his head again. "Seemed a bit dodgy," he repeated.

"Perhaps," said Maria, a little uncertainly, "you'd like to have a cup of tea and talk about it?"

"I could go for coffee," Sandy grinned.

Sandy and Maria had coffee together often after that night, at first at the café, then later at Maria's house. Sandy lived out of his office on the Goat Farm, and he enjoyed spending his evenings with Maria. Her house was comfortable and homey. They would sit together on the sofa or, when the mosquitoes were not bad, on her front porch. Not a few eyebrows were raised by their friendship, but most people considered it fitting that the two strangest people in Espantosa should become friends.

It was quite natural that one night Sandy should stand at the door, his hat in hand, and Maria, barefoot and smiling, should turn her face to his as he leaned forward and kissed her. And it was not long before people noted that Sandy could often been seen leaving Maria's house in the early hours of the morning.

It was about time, most of them said.

One day Sandy received an unusual visitor at the Goat Farm. He was seated behind his desk poring over contracts when his manager, Hector Garza, walked in, took off his coat, poured a cup of coffee and sat down heavily in the chair across from his employer and began to quietly unlace one of his boots. Sandy glanced up at the manager and waited.

"We got trouble, boss," said Hector, pulling off his other boot.

"Trouble?" said Sandy. He liked and trusted Hector, but he knew the man had a tendency to worry too much.

"There's someone here to see you."

"Send him in," said Sandy impatiently.

"It's not a him."

Sandy's ears perked up. "Who is it?"

"A woman."

"I got that," said Sandy.

"A woman named Guadalupe."

Sandy leaned back in his chair. He knew there was nothing he could do to speed things up, that if he demonstrated impatience Hector would only draw things out further. He waited.

"This woman," said Hector, putting his boot back on and drawing up the laces, "is no good. She's a bruja."

"A what?"

"A witch."

Sandy laughed out loud. "Then by all means send her in! I could do with a little excitement."

Hector appeared hurt. "No, boss, she's really a witch, and no damn good. If you see her, and you make her angry, she'll put a spell on you."

"Then I better get on her good side, eh, mate?"

"I'm serious, boss."

Sandy could see that he was, and he knew enough about local customs to realize it was better to humor the man. "Okay," he said soberly. "Send her in and I'll watch my step."

"Just be careful," said Hector, as he went to the door.

Sandy shuffled a few papers on his desk and jotted down a note. A moment later, the door opened.

The woman who came in was short and a little on the heavy side. She wore a dark green dress and heavy brogans. She had long, dark hair and deep black eyes. Sandy put her age at about forty, about the same age as Maria. She was not unattractive, though he noted she had dark hair on her cinnamon-colored arms, and a mole on her cheek from which there sprouted three short hairs. Sandy got to his feet to welcome her.

"Hello," he said, walking around the desk to meet her. He extended his hand and she took it. Her hand was very warm.

"I've come to tell you something," said the woman. "You have trouble."

"Please sit down," said Sandy. "I didn't catch your name."

"My name is Guadalupe Lopez," the woman announced, "and you have trouble."

Sandy sat down behind his desk. "It's good of you to come and tell me," he said. "What kind of trouble?"

The woman shook her head. "You need my help."

"You see, if you don't tell me what the trouble is, how can I judge whether or not I need your help, Miss Lopez?"

"They will all die," said Guadalupe. "Or some will die, and the rest you will kill. That is the trouble. Now you need my help?"

"What are you talking about?" Sandy felt uneasy. "I'm not gonna kill anybody."

"The goats," said Guadalupe. "You are going to kill them all."

"What?" Sandy exclaimed.

"No," Guadalupe corrected herself. "You will not kill them all. That is wrong. Some will die, the rest you will kill. I saw them."

The woman was obviously crazy, and he made a mental note to chew Hector out for letting her into his office. He had seen craziness in many forms, but this was something different, and altogether more upsetting.

"I saw them in a dream." Guadalupe leaned forward and lowered her voice. "They were burning."

Sandy felt like the temperature in the room had risen by several degrees. "That's ridiculous," he said.

"I can help you. But you have to do as I say."

Sandy stood up. He had enough of this. He resisted the impulse to throw the woman out on her ear. He said quietly and calmly, "I thank you for your offer. I will think about it and let you know."

"There is not much time," Guadalupe warned. "So don't think too long, or else they will all burn."

"Thank you," Sandy repeated.

Guadalupe rose to her feet. "If you think too long, they will all be dead. It will happen soon."

"I understand," said Sandy.

Guadalupe shrugged her shoulders and left. Sandy waited long enough for her to be out of earshot, then he opened the door and shouted, "Hector! Get in here!"

Sandy told Hector what Guadalupe said. At first, he was angry that the woman had even been allowed into his office, but as he told the story he found it all amusing. Hector listened in silence, and when Sandy was done, he shook his head and said, "Boss, you better listen to her."

"What?" said Sandy incredulously. "What the hell are you talking about?"

"You better do as she says," Hector repeated.

"For God's sake why?"

Hector stared down at his boots. "If you don't, something might happen."

"Like what?"

"I don't know. But if I were you, I'd listen to her."

"Well, it's a damn good thing you're not me, then. The goats are perfectly healthy. We had an inspection not ten days ago. Don't you think if there was anything wrong with them they'd have found it? Besides, even if something was wrong, what could that woman do about it?"

"I don't know."

"It's nothing but a poor attempt at extortion, plain and simple. She must take me for a damn fool."

That night, as he lay in bed with Maria, Sandy told her about his visit from Guadalupe. To his surprise, Maria seemed to take the matter seriously.

"What did she want you to do?" she asked.

"What does it matter?"

"I just wondered."

"You can't be telling me you take that woman seriously?"

Maria rolled over onto her back and looked up at the ceiling. "I know it sounds foolish, but I've heard stories about that woman. People say she's a bruja, a witch."

"You can't believe that!"

"No," said Maria, but there was an unmistakable uncertainty in her voice. "But I know there's things in life you can't explain. A lot of strange things happen around that woman. I just think it would be better to be safe than sorry."

Sandy was quiet. He was disappointed in Maria. He had looked forward to telling her about the incident, feeling sure that she would be on his side. The thought that she was just as gullible as Hector upset him. He let the matter drop.

Yet over the next few days, Sandy closely examined the herd. He didn't know what he was looking for, and he felt like a fool looking for anything at all. Each inspection confirmed what Sandy already knew: everything was fine.

Hector watched his boss in silence. When Sandy would complete another round, he would look over at Hector and grin as if to say, See, I told you so. Hector only nodded agreeably and waited. Though he said no more about the affair, in the privacy of his thoughts he considered his boss a damn fool.

Not only was there no sign of the disaster Guadalupe predicted, things were going extremely well. Sandy was a good businessman. The Aussie Goat Farm was showing a healthy profit. He secured contracts with several school districts, and soon students in cafeterias throughout the region were sipping milk from cartons emblazoned with the Aussie label.

Guadalupe never returned, and after several weeks even Hector had to admit that perhaps his boss had been right after all.

One evening, as Sandy was driving into town after work, he stopped at a railroad crossing to watch a train pass. Never had he been able to look at a train without wanting to climb aboard. The wanderlust had hit him young. He had been on the move since the age of fifteen, when he dropped out of school to take a job on a ship bound for Singapore. Once he arrived in Singapore, Sandy jumped ship and never looked back. Now, as he watched the boxcars rumble by, he thought of climbing into bed with Maria, and for the first time in his life, he felt no desire to go with them.

As the last car in the train passed by and he slowly drove forward, Sandy Foster felt like he was going home.

If Maria felt that she had played only a supporting role in the brief and bitter saga of Tom Walsh's life, in her relationship with Sandy she felt she had finally won the lead. It wasn't the movie she'd dreamed of as a young girl, but she admitted that the role suited her well. And when Sandy proposed to her that evening, she didn't even hesitate in accepting. Afterwards, they made love, and as she lay in his arms she allowed herself to believe that fate had finally granted her what she had come to least expect: happiness.

The morning after he proposed to Maria, Sandy went to work as usual. He knew that something was wrong as soon as he got out of the car. Hector was standing outside the office, and several workers were gathered there also.

Hector walked over and said grimly, "Boss, we got trouble."

Sandy followed Hector to one of the pens and saw immediately that he was right. Several goats were lying on the ground in grotesque positions. They were all dead.

Sandy spent the next hour inspecting the rest of the herd. When he was satisfied that the remaining stock seemed healthy, he returned to the pen and examined the dead goats. "What about the feed? Any chance something got into it?"

"I fed them all the same," said Hector.

He looked about the pen for any sign of a contaminant. "It has to be something they ingested." But even as he said this he knew he was wrong.

Hector said nothing. Neither man wanted to admit what it could be.

Sandy gave the order to stop production and hold all shipments. Then he went inside and called the F.D.A. field office. By noon an agent and two vets appeared and examined the dead animals. Sandy paced at a distance. When the vets finished examining the bodies, the agent walked over, shaking his head.

"It's not good," he said. "It's hard to tell if it's spread to the rest of the stock. They'll have to be quarantined, of course. And you'll need to recall whatever product you have on the shelf."

Sandy nodded grimly.

"I'm sorry, Mr. Foster," said the agent, wiping his hand across his forehead, "but if it has spread you know what it means."

Sandy knew.

When Maria learned of the disaster, she drove out to the farm immediately. She found Sandy in his office. He was grim.

"The tests are back," he said. "They'll all have to be destroyed."

"Can't any of them be saved?"

"No."

Maria offered to stay, but Sandy insisted she go home. She did not see him again for several days. Then one afternoon as she was walking to the Rialto, she saw the dark plume of smoke rising on the horizon.

The smoke from the fires at the Aussie Goat Farm darkened the skies around Espantosa for nearly a week. Sandy himself oversaw the slaughter and the burning of the carcasses. If Hector was ever tempted to tell Sandy he should have listened to Guadalupe, he never did so. After the disposal was complete, he refused to take his last paycheck. He later said he had never seen a truly broken man until that day.

When it was all over, Sandy walked through the deserted farm. He felt numb. Worst of all, he didn't know how he was going to face Maria. He had made up his mind that he could not marry her until he managed to recover, if he ever did. The thought of living off her income, of licking his wounds in the same house he had once dared to think of as home was too much for him.

In the end, he didn't face her at all. He wrote a letter, and dropped it into a mailbox in the next town.

Maria never even opened the letter.

Chapter Nineteen

After Sandy's disappearance, Melchor retraced his steps. He woke Connie, who, though still queasy, agreed to drive him around town. Melchor stuck his head out the window of the car and called the dog. He only succeeded only in rousing every other dog in Espantosa. Finally, they were forced to admit defeat.

"It's no good," Connie said. "That dog is lost."

Lost. Even on the night he found Sandy, the dog did not appear to be lost. It was almost as if he had been waiting for Melchor that night in the dark.

"Okay," he agreed. "I guess we've done all we can."

As Connie drove him home, Melchor kept looking out the window. When they approached the Rialto, he half expected to see Sandy sitting out front, but there was no sign of him.

"We'll try again tomorrow," said Connie, laying a hand on his arm. "Maybe he'll show up during the night."

"Maybe so," he agreed half-heartedly.

Once inside, Melchor felt suddenly exhausted. He climbed up the stairs to his apartment and collapsed on the bed.

Melchor was wakened by the sound of pounding on the front door of the Rialto. He rolled out of bed and stumbled down the stairs, glancing at the clock as he went. It was three. He opened the door and Sandy bounded past him.

But Melchor's attention was drawn to the dim, shadowy figure outside. He peered into the dark, rubbing the sleep from his eyes. "Guadalupe?" he said tentatively.

"Why don't you keep that dog on a leash?" said the old woman, moving into the light.

Melchor laughed. Leashes were unheard of in Espantosa. "Where did you find him? I thought he was lost for good."

"Just 'cause you can't find something doesn't mean it's lost."

"I suppose so. Anyway, thanks for bringing Sandy home."

"Only a pendejo like you would name a negrito like this Sandy," said Guadalupe.

"I guess I named him after Sandy Foster. I found him out by the goat farm."

"It's not good to name animals after people.""

"It just seemed to fit. He came right away when I called him."

Guadalupe raised an eyebrow. "That man was cursed. Maybe you are, too. Or maybe it's the whole town."

"I don't believe in curses," said Melchor quietly.

"No," said Guadalupe, turning to leave. "But you will."

As the sun rose, Santiago ate his tacos, licking the egg yolk off his fingers, and gazed at the restored bleachers across the field. Freshly painted the day before, they gleamed in the morning sun, and seeing them in that light, he was inclined to be more generous toward God.

"All right, you bastrard," he said, "maybe the lumber was a gift, after all."

He turned to the pile of ragged lumber he'd stacked behind the bleachers. He bent over and picked up one of the planks. It was warped and splintered. Then he remembered the platform stage. "This lumber is not so bad, que no?" He began to remove the nails from the plank. "And these nails are still good, too," he added, holding up the rusted nail to the light. "No point in letting it all go to waste."

After removing the nails, Santiago went to fetch a truck. He loaded the lumber and drove down to the old bowling alley.

He had never built a platform stage before, and Melchor had provided no directions on what he wanted. He stared at the empty lot and scratched his head. "Well," he said, "a platform stage is just a platform, que no? I just have to raise it off the ground." Santiago picked up his saw, chose one of the better planks, and started to work.

Santiago could work quickly when he wanted to, and he was anxious to finish the stage before that fool Mayor came around to inspect it. Once it was done, he would slap some paint on it and no one would be the wiser.

Still, it took until past noon for him to finish. He stepped back and surveyed the stage. It stood about six inches above the ground. It was about eight feet long and almost as wide. He put one foot on the stage and tested it. It seemed sound, at least toward the edges, where the supports were. He had wanted to build a support in the middle, but the lumber was really much worse than he had thought and several of the planks splintered as soon as he began to drive the nail in. He threw the scraps back into the truck and took out a can of paint. He had used the paint Melchor had given him on the bleachers, and had been forced to scrounge around for more. All he found in the end was half a gallon of orange and half a gallon of green, the school colors. Both cans were so ancient he had to pry their lids off with a hammer and chisel. Inside, the paint was thick and pasty. He poured the paints together, added some thinner, and produced a slimy, puke-colored mixture.

When the job was complete, Santiago stepped back and looked it over. He had told himself that this kind of a stage was all that idiot fake Mayor deserved, but in his heart he felt bad. He took pride in his work, and what he saw in front of him made him feel ashamed. He wiped a hand across his forehead and sighed.

He drove back to the school with a heavy heart, but when he saw the bleachers again, he felt better. "It's a bad wind that doesn't blow somebody good," he said. Then, a little confused about what this meant, he added, "It's no use crying over spilled milk." But this, too, seemed to confuse him. Finally, he simply said, "It's all for the best, si Dios quiere." Satisfied at last, he headed home.

When Melchor heard that the stage had been completed, he went immediately to inspect it. Connie, still pale and shaky from the night before, accompanied him.

"What the hell is that?" said Melchor, as they approached the stage. "It looks like.... well, I don't know what it looks like, but it sure doesn't look like a stage. It's barely even off the ground!"

Connie had to agree that the stage was a disappointment. "It might not even matter," she said. "I got a call this morning. Jorge Boca canceled."

"What? The day before the festival?" Boca was the last of a long line of musical "headliners" that Connie had been trying to enlist for the past two weeks. Melchor put one foot on the stage and felt it shiver. He tried to step up, and it groaned. "Maybe it's just as well," he said. "No way this thing would support Boca." Boca was a once popular conjunto singer who had added considerable weight once his career began to fizzle. It was rumored that he weighed close to four hundred pounds. "We'll just have to make do with Herbie," Melchor added somberly.

Connie sighed, "There's no way Herbie can play the entire time."

"Okay, okay," said Melchor, turning to leave. "We'll just have to find someone else."

"Not at this point."

"I'll think of something." Melchor looked back over his shoulder at the stage. He shook his head sadly.

As they walked down the street, he said to Connie, "I've been thinking. We should have a meeting."

Connie laughed. One of the things Melchor had been famous for in the months immediately following his "election" was that he was constantly holding meetings. That almost no one ever attended these meetings did not seem to deter him. "I want input from the People," he would say, careful to capitalize the "P" even in speech. Then one day, at a meeting to discuss his "Friendly Face" campaign– an initiative to improve the town's relations with out-of-town visitors– Melchor realized the People were sending him a message, loud and clear: their silence was deafening.

"I know, I know," Melchor admitted. "But we need to discuss what we're going to do tomorrow. I want to make sure we're all on the same page. I was thinking we could meet at the Rialto."

Connie considered this for a moment. "Hold it at the Beer Haus."

"Why the Beer Haus?"

"Because people will be more likely to attend if they know they can wash down a speech with a cold beer."

Melchor laughed. "I don't plan to make a speech. I just want everyone to know what's expected of them."

"It's a good idea. I'll pass the word along."

"I thought we could each take a list of names and call them. Then we could visit those folks who don't have phones, and..."

"Melchor! This is Espantosa. You could whisper it to a telephone pole and everyone would know about it in an hour."

"I guess you're right."

"Of course I'm right. There are no secrets here. Take you and me, for instance."

Melchor stopped. "You and me?"

Connie rolled her eyes. "The whole town is talking about us."

"What?"

"They've practically married us off already."

Melchor was dumbfounded. "I had no idea." Then it occurred to him that Connie might find all this talk uncomfortable. "I'm sorry," he added.

"Oh, I don't mind," said Connie shyly. Melchor looked at her, but her eyes were on the pavement at their feet.

They arrived at the door to the Tumbleweed Café and Connie, who had promised Roy to come in that afternoon, paused. She glanced down the street. "The town looks nice," she said.

Melchor followed her gaze. "Yeah," he said absentmindedly. "Listen, I'm sorry about the rumors."

"Hell, I don't care. People are gonna talk anyway. Besides," she glanced at him briefly, "a girl could do worse."

Melchor laughed. "It's nice to know I'm not the absolute bottom of the barrel."

Connie blushed. "I didn't mean that."

"I know."

Connie looked over her shoulder. The café was enjoying a good lunch crowd. The diners were trying hard to make it obvious they weren't staring at the two of them.

"If people are gonna talk," she said, drawing close, "we might as well give them something to talk about." She gave him a fleeting kiss and, smiling, went inside.

Melchor watched her disappear behind the counter. He glanced at the diners inside. Fent Hurley, his fork paused in midair, was staring open-mouthed. Mrs. Nelson leaned over and whispered to her son, who had his back to the scene. He turned and stared at Melchor. Roy, who had been leaning over the counter, seemed frozen on the spot. Melchor noticed none of this.

He was fighting the impulse to follow Connie inside. Then, overcoming this urge, he turned and began to walk briskly down the street. Sandy trotted beside him, happily nipping at his heels.

Connie was right. The town *did* look brighter. The windows of the Sears Catalogue Center, long caked with yellow grime, had been polished and gleamed brightly in the afternoon sun. Even the Rialto looked respectable. Melchor could not remember a time, since his childhood, when the town looked so nice.

At the end of the street, the Titan Football team was attempting to hang a banner across the road between two telephone poles. As Melchor approached, they finished tying the banner in place. The players at the top of the poles gave a weak holler and began to climb down.

"It's facing the wrong way," said Melchor.

"What?" Mr. Wilkins, the football coach, was sitting on the curb, sipping a coke and eating pork rinds. He was a big-bellied man with very little hair that he combed forward in a failed attempt to hide his bald spot. "Why's it the wrong way? Everyone can see it."

"Yeah," said Melchor, "but isn't the idea that people see it on the way into town? Isn't that why it says 'Welcome?'"

Wilkins stared at the banner. The boys stared at it, too. "Oh, hell. Let's turn it around boys."

"Also, it's prairie oysters, not otters."

"Eh?"

"Your sign says Prairie Otters."

"That's right. Prairie Otters."

"It's supposed to say Prairie Oysters."

219

"Prairie oysters?" said the coach. "What the hell are those?"

Chapter Twenty

The lights in the Rialto dimmed promptly at eight o'clock. The beam of light summoned up the usual spirits which stuttered across the screen. Melchor rarely watched the movie any more, but for some reason tonight he felt like seeing it again. He took a seat in the middle of the theater and tried to concentrate on the film, resisting the urge to fill in the missing portions that he'd been forced to snip out over the years. He wondered vaguely if all the edits, forced by the deterioration could actually be, subtly, improvements. What if, each time he was forced to snip another few feet, he was creating a wholly new interpretation of the original? Soon, however, he realized the storyline was completely garbled; it simply made no sense any more.

Gradually he lost interest in the movie, distracted by the sounds of the kids making out in the darkness. He failed to notice the door swing open behind him and the solitary figure that entered. It was several minutes before he realized someone was sitting across the aisle from him. He bent over and studied the face in the darkness. It was Miss Coakely.

He watched her for some time. She did not appear to notice him. Surprisingly, she seemed actually to be interested in the movie.

Then, as he watched, he saw one pale hand move slowly between her legs. It disappeared under her trousers. After a few moments, her head tilted back and he could see her face clearly. Her eyes were closed and her lips parted. Her shoulders shook and then relaxed.

It was only then that she looked around and saw him. She looked at him for a solid minute, then rose and left the theater. Melchor followed her quickly.

He found her standing beside the counter in front of the popcorn machine.

"What were you doing in there?" Melchor asked.

"Masturbating," she said matter-of-factly. "Isn't that what people do in theaters?"

"No," said Melchor. "I mean, not in Espantosa."

"Oh, so it's okay to fuck but not to masturbate. Didn't you see those kids fucking?"

Melchor cleared his throat. "I didn't notice," he lied.

"Of course you did. I bet you jerk off watching them do it. You're the type." She glared at Melchor. "And that print is a piece of shit."

"I'm know."

"It's okay. I got what I came for. I can't do anything in the Pastor's house because he's always listening outside the door."

"Pastor Gill?"

"Bastard Gill more like it. You know, he came on to me the first night I was there. I told him to blow it out his ass."

Melchor was surprised by the sudden rush of confidences. "Does Mrs. Gill know?"

"I think she does. That's why she wants me to stay. He tried to kick me out, but she won't let him."

"Why would she want you to stay?"

"To bug him, of course. It's her way of punishing him, I think. There's more to that lady than meets the eye."

"I guess so."

Melchor took the money from the till and carried it into the office where he placed it in the bag of quarters he'd collected from the Soft Soap that afternoon. When he turned around, Miss Coakely was standing in the doorway.

"Why haven't you?"

"Why haven't I what?"

"Come on to me. Everyone else in town has. Especially that Gorman guy. He gives me the creeps. You can't tell me you haven't thought about it. She reached into the cooler and pulled out a soda. "Your cokes are hot," she said. "You have any ice?"

"Upstairs."

She motioned for him to lead the way. Melchor led her up the stairs. He opened the door and turned on the light. The girl walked over to the window and looked down at the darkened street. He put some ice in a glass, and handed it to her

"You can see the whole town from up here," she said. "God, what a piece of shit!"

"Is that what you're going to say in your book?"

"The book?" She sipped her coke. "I have to say positive things in the book."

"But you said the Rialto should be torn down."

"That's what I think, but I can't write that. Listen, do you mind if I crash here tonight? I really can't face Bastard Gill again."

Melchor hesitated. He was unsure of what to make of the sudden change in Miss Coakely. He also wondered how Connie would react if she learned she had spent the night in his apartment. He could make a fair guess. He looked over his shoulder at the bed. "There's a cot in the projection room."

"A cot?" Miss Coakely looked at the bed.

Melchor swallowed hard. "I guess you can have the bed."

"Suit yourself. Where's the bathroom?"

Melchor pointed at the door. Miss Coakely fished a make-up bag out of her backpack and left the room.

He waited a moment, then quickly reached down and picked up her bag. He peered inside. There it was. The Book.

He opened it.

At first, he couldn't make any sense of it. The handwriting was so small and cramped that it almost seemed to be written in a foreign language. He carried the book over to the light. Gradually, he mastered her handwriting. He was able to make out the first page.

It certainly didn't look like a guidebook. He turned the page. Then he turned another. It was the same throughout, pages and pages of scribbled notes, mostly personal stuff, some poetry even. One page contained a recipe for Mrs. Gills famous lemon tarts. He came across a page devoted to sexual fantasies involving someone he had never heard of but who seemed to be a rock star or something. Conspicuously absent from the book was even a single description of the town or its inhabitants. He scanned the last pages quickly. The final entry was a long and somewhat obscene poem about a dog and a cat sleeping together. Melchor supposed it was meant to be funny. He replaced the notebook in the backpack and turned toward the window.

"If you don't mind, I'm going to turn in," said Miss Coakely, emerging from the bathroom. She unbuttoned her trousers and slipped them off. She wore no panties. Melchor stared at her dumbfounded, but she continued to undress unselfconsciously.

"I have to go turn off the projector," he said thickly.

"Goodnight," said Miss Coakely.

He walked to the door as she slipped off her blouse, revealing her breasts, which were small, with tiny nipples the color of strawberries.

Melchor closed the door. He stood with his hand on the doorknob for several minutes, considering the erotic possibilities. Then his mind went back to the Book. It was all a lie. There was no guidebook. This simple fact amazed him. Even the thought of a woman lying naked in his own bed on the other side of the door could not shake from his mind that single, overwhelming thought: There was no guidebook! Melchor went to the projection booth and turned off the projector. He turned up the house lights slowly. In the theater, several teenage couples hastily assembled their clothing and left, smiling at each other as they did.

Sitting down on the cot, he unlaced his shoes. Then he remembered he still had to lock up and walked down the stairs in his socks.

He checked the theater, turned off the lights and went to lock the door. He stepped out into the night air, took a long look at the dark and empty street. The lights of the jukebox across the street shone through the café window. The neon beer sign on the wall of the pool hall gave the place an eerie, otherworldly glow. In the distance, he heard the sound of a train.

Suddenly it all made sense. He wondered how many times she'd done it? Did she move from town to town, spinning the same tale? Yes, that must be what she did. He thought about the stories everyone had been feeding her, hoping in vain to get just a few lines in the Book. Then he laughed out loud, a deep, sonorous laugh that could be heard halfway across town.

Melchor woke with a bad crick in his neck. He sat up and stared at his feet. It was several minutes before he recalled the events of the night before. He dressed quickly, went to the door of his apartment, and knocked. There was no reply. He knocked again, then opened it. The room was empty.

He was not surprised. He had never really expected to find her still there.

He went downstairs and entered his office. He sat down heavily on the chair. Then, as he looked at the shelf beside the desk, his jaw dropped.

The bag of quarters was gone.

By afternoon, news of Miss Coakely's departure had spread throughout town. Reactions varied, but most people, free of the concern over what she might or might not say in the Book, took the opportunity to sum up against the girl.

"I never liked her," said Mrs. Nelson. "She was as rude as the day is long."

"That girl," said Roy, "ate here at least once a day every day and she never once said thank you."

Bill French summed it up this way: "She rode into town on an empty tank. I'm betting she left the same way, like a thief in the night."

Connie offered the most scathing criticism of all. "I'd rather have Typhoid Mary come to town than the likes of Miss Amanda Coakely."

The one person with nothing to say on the issue was Pastor Gill. The previous night he had lain in bed for a long time after he heard the sound of Miss Coakely's car starting. He had no need to check her room. He knew she was gone. He closed his eyes and tried to force from his mind the image of the girl. His wife snored softly beside him. He reached out and touched her shoulder. His touch roused her, and she turned away from him.

He waited until her breathing became regular once more, then slipped out of bed and walked to the front porch. The air was warm and humid. He walked across the grass in his bare feet and stared down the empty road.

Miss Coakely's departure, he realized, changed nothing. Her spirit would inhabit the house for weeks, maybe months, a constant reminder of his failure as a husband. Worse still, her absence gave him no opportunity for atonement. He could not put the matter right.

He felt like a man who had been standing on the edge of a precipice. He had stared into the chasm, feeling that at any moment he might topple forward to his ruin. Now, he found that the precipice had disappeared. In its place was a landscape of utter desolation. He had never felt more alone. He sank to his knees in the dewy grass. He put his hands together and attempted to pray, but he could not mouth the words. All he could manage was a hoarse whisper: "Dear God, forgive me."

At that moment, as though in answer to his half-formed prayer, the sound of laughter reached his ears. It was a deep, sonorous laugh devoid of gaiety. To the Pastor, the sound was filled with unspeakable irony. It was like a slap in the face from God himself.

He rose with difficulty and walked back to the house. He opened the front door and entered, feeling like a stranger in his own home.

The next morning, in the light of day, he found himself moving restlessly from room to room. He said nothing to his wife about Miss Coakely's departure, and she did not seem to have noticed. Her only acknowledgment came when she went to the room to collect the bedding. As she carried the sheets into the washroom, she said to her husband, "I think it was unwise to allow Miss Coakely to drink coffee in her room." She showed him a large brown spot on one of the sheets. "I believe," she added, picking up the iron, "that this will leave a stain for a long time to come."

Chapter Twenty-One

"Don't you smoke, boy?"

Gorman Price glared at the apparition on his toilet and shook his head.

"I never trusted a man who didn't smoke," said the former President. He cast a disapproving look toward Gorman. "Damn, I could use a good cigar right now. You sure you haven't got one?"

"I'm sure," said Gorman through gritted teeth.

"Every man's got vices. What's yours?"

Gorman didn't answer. He was seated on the floor in the hallway. Beside him lay several empty cans of air freshener and an industrial size bottle of Lysol, also empty. It had been nearly a week since the former President had taken up permanent residence in his bathroom. In that time, Gorman had been unable to convince the apparition to vacate the room except when Gorman himself needed to use the facilities. Even then, the spirit was testy.

"All right, but don't take all day about it," he groused.

Gorman had been unable to shower and he could no longer distinguish between his own body odor and the sump-like stench that permeated the whole house.

"Couldn't you go out and buy a cigar?"

"No."

The spirit looked at him slyly. "A good smoke always helps me go."

Gorman had been staring dejectedly at his feet. At this, he looked up. "Really?" he asked dubiously.

"Yep. A good smoke always kept me regular."

Gorman got to his feet. "Okay, but on one condition."

"Everyone's got conditions." The ghost shook his head. "Name it."

"If I get you a cigar, you have to go."

"Well, that's the damn idea, isn't it?"

"I mean you have to leave."

L.B.J. paused. "All right. But I get to finish my smoke."

Gorman slipped on his shoes and was already at the door when the spirit called after him, "And don't buy none of those dime-store cheapies, you hear?"

By seven-thirty that night, people began to arrive at the Beer Haus. By eight, the place was packed. Nearly everyone in Espantosa, even those who weren't directly involved, had shown up. In fact, the only person who was late was Melchor. When he finally arrived, the crowd had broken up into small groups around the bar and the pool tables. Some people had drifted out back to the deck, where Herbie Menchaca, who had confused the meeting with the festival itself, was eking out polkas on his accordion.

When Melchor tried to call the meeting to order, Oscar Escalante shouted from the back of the room, "Hang a minute, primo, I need to run the table on this pendejo."

Melchor looked at Connie and shrugged.

The meeting for the First Annual Prairie Oyster Festival would go down in history as one of the best parties ever held in Espantosa. It was one of the highest grossing nights in Beer Haus history, second only to the Hang Dicky by the Balls soiree held after news of Nixon's resignation, an impromptu shindig which crossed party lines and lasted more than three days.

"Melchor," said Connie, "don't you think we should talk about the festival?"

He belched, "Why interrupt them now? Everyone is having such a good time."

And it was true. Rarely had the citizens of Espantosa gathered together in an atmosphere of such good will and fellowship. By ten o'clock, Tomás Cruz had shown up with his bass and even little Jesse Jenkins was dragged out of bed and enlisted to play drums. Throughout the evening, Herbie squeezed out corridos, polkas, and the occasional ranchera. Even Pastor Gill and Mrs. Gill took a turn on the dance floor, the Pastor smiling as he tried to waltz to a corrido.

By midnight the party was still going strong, even though Rudy had sold out of every kind of beer. Several citizens took up a collection and drove to the Pak-N-Sip for twelve packs, and when they returned the party continued unabated.

"Hey, Melchor," said a voice behind him. He turned. It was Mr. Roycroft. "What the hell are Prairie Oysters?"

"Bull testicles," said Melchor.

"Bull's balls? You're kidding!"

"Nope. That's what they are."

"Well I'll be damned." He walked away shaking his head.

Oscar Escalante stumbled over to Melchor and slapped him on the back.

"You know, primo," he said thickly, "I gotta hand it to you. This is a hell of a party."

Melchor winced and rubbed his shoulder. "Great," he said.

"Let me buy you a cerveza, primo," said Oscar, grabbing Melchor by the arm.

It was a half hour before Melchor managed to tear himself away from his cousin. He found Connie seated in a booth and slid in opposite her.

"Quite a shindig," said Connie.

"It's what this town needed."

Melchor stared down at the table for a moment. "There's something I need to tell you," he said, lowering his voice.

"What is it?"

He leaned forward. "Before Miss Coakely disappeared, she stayed at my place."

Connie raised an eyebrow. "I see."

"No, no. It's nothing like that," Melchor protested.

"Uh huh." Connie gave him a cold glare.

"I promise you nothing happened. I slept on the cot." He gave her such an earnest look that Connie finally had to laugh despite herself.

"It's just that I happened to get a look at the Book."

"Really?"

"Yes."

"Well?"

Melchor glanced around the room nervously. "There was nothing in it. I mean, nothing about the town."

"Oh, my Lord." Connie gave a low whistle.

"Yeah. It was full of all kinds of stuff, but there's one thing for sure," his voice sank to a whisper, "she was never writing a guidebook. It was all a fraud."

Connie threw back her head and laughed. "Well, I'll be damned!" She slapped the table with her open hand. "I knew it! I knew that girl was up to no good."

"I guess so," said Melchor painfully. "The trouble is, how do I tell everyone?"

Connie looked around the room. "Maybe you shouldn't say anything. After a while maybe, but not tonight."

"People are bound to find out."

"Maybe. Then again they might not. Anyway, I doubt it'll matter that much in the end."

"What?"

"It's like you said. Look at them. This festival has really brought people together. You know, it's really an amazing thing. We're all so different. In a big city, these people would never even know each other. Mr. Rigby would never get into an argument with Fent Hurley about fertilization. I mean, it would never be a conversation. In a big city, it would all be handled by committees, and no one would ever talk, I mean really talk about it."

Melchor agreed. "Kind of gives you hope, doesn't it?"

Connie spread her hands on the table. "Yes, it does," she said firmly.

"You know," he said, "things have never gone well in this town for long, but I got the feeling our luck is about to change."

BOOM!!!

"What the FUCK was that?" Oscar Escalante shouted.

Everyone scrambled for the doors. Once outside, there was a collective gasp from the crowd. A few blocks away, the sky was bright with red and orange flames.

"Holy shit!" exclaimed little Jesse Jenkins.

Gorman Price had been forced to drive all the way to Carrizo Springs to purchase the cigar. The Pak-N-Sip carried only Swisher Sweets and he didn't want to risk offending his unwelcome guest.

When he returned to the house, he took one last gulp of air and opened the door. The stench hit him like a ton of rotten cabbage. He stumbled inside, gasping and choking.

"Did you get my smokes?" called a voice from the restroom.

"Yes," Gorman said, coughing. He staggered into the restroom and handed the cigar to the ghost.

The spirit rolled the cigar in his fingers and sniffed it delicately. "This the best you could do?" he sneered.

"One dollar and fifty-five cents," said Gorman, sinking to the floor in the hall.

"Shit. Well, it'll have to do." He looked at Gorman expectantly. "Got a light?"

"What? Oh." Gorman searched his pockets.

"Can't very well smoke it without lighting it, boy."

Gorman, his head swimming, got to his feet and stumbled into the kitchen. He searched through drawers and finally found a matchbook. Inside was one match. He took this back to the bathroom and tossed it onto the floor. "There's only one," he said.

"That's fine. I can light a cigar in a snowstorm."

Gorman felt like he might vomit at any moment. "I'm going outside," he said.

"Fine. I'll be done in no time."

Gorman walked unsteadily to the front door, threw it open, and sank to his knees on the front porch.

Inside the restroom, the spirit licked the end of the cigar, placed it in his mouth, and struck the match.

Gorman, bent double with the dry heaves, never even heard the explosion. The next thing he knew, there was a bright flash and he was thrown head first across the lawn where he fell with a bone-crunching thud.

The first people to arrive on the scene found Gorman unconscious. Behind him, his house, what was left of it, blazed like a Roman candle, sending sparks into the air a hundred feet. Once it was ascertained Gorman was not dead, people turned their attention to preventing the fire from spreading. Jimmy Falcon, arriving with the volunteer fire company, took one look at Gorman's house and turned his hoses on the neighboring structures. So many sparks showered down upon the onlookers that Fent Hurley was briefly set ablaze. He was doused in time to prevent serious injury.

"My God," said Roy, "the roof's blown clear off."

The roof was located several days later, nearly a mile from the scene.

Connie and Melchor stood together some distance from the inferno.

"What could've caused an explosion like that?" Connie said in awe.

Melchor rubbed his chin. "Gas?" he offered.

It was close to three in the morning when the blaze finally burned down and was deemed to no longer be a threat to neighboring houses. Though the ruins would smolder for several days, Jimmy Falcon pronounced the fire under control and people began to stagger toward their homes, drunk and exhausted. Many had continued drinking during the conflagration, offering up beer from the tailgates of pick-up trucks. Things got so merry at one point that Herbie Menchaca, who had rushed out of the Beer Haus accordion in hand, began to squeeze out a polka, until Leroy Polk told him to stop acting like a damn fool.

Gorman Price recovered consciousness and began to mumble incoherently. Bending over him, Bill French tried to question him about the accident. Leroy Polk walked over, brushing soot off his hat. "Well?" he asked.

"I think he's still out of it," said French, shaking his head. "Claims the explosion was caused by L.B.J."

"Oh, hell!" Polk spat. "Somebody better haul his sorry ass over to a doctor."

Guadalupe Lopez was staring at the blue and white flecks of light that danced across the TV screen in front of her when the explosion rattled the windows of her house. She had been awake all night, and though she tried to relax, she was tense in body and spirit. She was waiting, but for what she did not know. She only knew what she expected would not be long in coming. When the explosion finally happened, only then did her body relax. She rubbed her hand across her eyes and let out a long, low breath.

"Ah," she muttered, rising from the great armchair and scattering sunflower seeds onto the floor, "at last."

She shuffled out the front door of the house. Already people were in the street, gazing up at the sparks swirling in the dark sky above Espantosa. Some piled into their pickup trucks and raced off to witness the disaster first hand. Guadalupe leaned on a post and shook her head.

She was very tired. With an effort, she lowered herself onto the steps of her front porch. She could taste the ash in the air. It reminded her of another time, when the smell of smoke was not so sweet. She thought of Sandy Foster and that pendejo Melchor Mendoza. They were two of a kind. But she had liked Foster. Maybe she even liked Mendoza.

A flood of memories rushed into her mind, of herself as a young girl, and of her mother. She thought she could hear her wailing faintly in the night even now, like a soul lost in the darkness. She thought of her father and his pitiful faith in his nopal. And then a succession of images raced by, the faces of the children she had brought into the world, and the faces of the old that had faded from the memory of the living, as she would in time. She saw the town as it used to be, and then, in rapid succession, saw buildings rise and fall as though with each breath the town was created and then destroyed, and she saw also her own body transformed by age, her hands, once smooth and delicate, seemed to age and wrinkle before her eyes, and her own face stared back at her from the long passage of years, and it seemed to her she and the town had aged together, and their fate was one, and through it all there was a single constant, one body that remained and remained unchanged: the lake, the lake around which the tiny town had struggled, grown and subsided and whose waters flowed even now in her veins and those of her townspeople. It was the longest story of her life and though she tried she could not see the end. Then again in her mind she was hovering over the town, spreading her giant wings, looking down on all she had ever loved or hated, and her heart was filled now with a deep, abiding pity for everyone she had ever known. And then the visions passed, leaving her once more simply an old, tired woman.

She rose unsteadily and looked up at the night sky. Some people said destiny was written in the stars. Guadalupe had never believed this. The animal within her knew that her fate and the fate of her people were sealed beneath the dark, brooding waters of the Espantosa.

One of the few residents who did not witness the fire first hand was Santiago. The explosion shook his tiny shack and rattled windows almost out of their frames. Santiago never stirred. A few hours later, when he got up to pee, he heard music outside and went to investigate.

Herbie Menchaca was leading a line of drunken revelers across the football field, squeezing out a corrido as they danced and staggered home. A fine ash was settling over the town, and as the dancers approached the security light by the bus garage, they took on a ghostly appearance. At that distance, to Santiago's sleepy eyes, it looked much as if Death himself was leading the parade. Following the line of dancers at some distance was a tall figure in a white Stetson who with arms raised leapt lightly off the ground, pirouetted and balanced delicately in the air for an unnatural time before descending once more to the earth.

Santiago watched until the revelers disappeared, then raised his eyes to heaven. "All right, you son-of-a-bitch," he mumbled, "you win." Then he added, for no apparent reason, "It's better to light a candle than to curse at the dark." Satisfied that this summed up his experience well, he went back inside his shack and fell into deep and untroubled sleep.

The sun rose over the unconscious town. The conflagration of the night before had left behind a sickly yellow haze that seeped in through every door and pried into the nooks and crannies of every home. So noxious was this ether that it might well have claimed the lives of half the inhabitants if not for a saving wind, the heavy sigh perhaps of some obscure deity, that swept through the streets of Espantosa and ruffled briefly the sad banner of the first and final Prairie Otter Festival.

Some of the residents failed to make it home that night; they collapsed in the street where, covered by the fine ash, they resembled the frozen figures of Pompeii.